F

THE CHOCOLATE LOVER

M.E. Rabb (the "M" stands for Margo) was born in Manhattan, raised in Queens, and now lives in Brooklyn, New York, with her husband, Marshall, and their asthmatic cat. She has published short stories and essays in various American magazines, including *Seventeen*, *The Atlantic Monthly* and *Mademoiselle*. *The Rose Queen* is the first novel in the Missing Persons series, and her first title for Walker Books.

Visit her online at www.merabb.com

Other titles in the Missing Persons series:

MISSING PERSONS

Case #2:
The Chocolate Lover

M.E. Rabb

WALKER BOOKS
AND SUBSIDIARIES

LONDON · BOSTON · SYDNEY · AUCKLAND

Acknowledgements

Thank you to Marshall Reid, Jackie Rabb, Liesa Abrams,
Kristin Gilson, Sara Shandler, and Mara Bergman
for their help with this book.

Published by arrangement with Puffin Books,
a division of Penguin Group (USA) Inc.
This edition published 2005 by Walker Books Ltd
87 Vauxhall Walk, London SE11 5HJ
2 4 6 8 10 9 7 5 3 1
Copyright © 2004 by 17th Street Productions,
an Alloy company and M.E. Rabb
Cover photo © Getty Images
The right of M.E. Rabb to be identified as author
of this work has been asserted by her in accordance
with the Copyright, Designs and Patents Act 1988
This book has been typeset in Optima
Printed and bound in Great Britain by Cox & Wyman Ltd, Reading, Berkshire
British Library Cataloguing in Publication Data:
a catalogue record for this book
is available from the British Library
ISBN 1-84428-141-8
www.walkerbooks.co.uk

For Julien Yoo,
from our number 7 train days
through eighteen years of
friendship and counting

Chicago Sentinel

April 25, 1947

MISSING

REWARD FOR INFORMATION
PLEASE HELP FIND
MISS RUTH BRAUNER

I am trying to locate Miss Ruth Rivka Brauner. She was last seen at Hester Klein's Boarding House for Women at 520 N. Michigan Avenue at seven o'clock in the evening on April 22, 1947. She is twenty-three years old with brown hair and brown eyes, five feet four inches tall with a slender figure. All persons with information regarding her whereabouts are requested to contact Mr. Leo Shattenberg at 1468 N. Milwaukee Avenue, Chicago, Illinois, or call CR7-2119.

1

"Don't leave me here," I pleaded with my sister, Sam. Our clanking, smoking, ancient brown Buick idled in the parking lot of Venice High. Sam and I had lived in Venice for almost two months, but today was my first day of tenth grade. I stared up at the sprawling brick building surrounded by cornfields; record-high heat had blanketed Indiana, and my legs stuck to the hot leather car seat like they were coated in Elmer's glue. I hadn't been this nervous about starting school since my first day of kindergarten at PS 11 in Queens, New York. My mom had walked me down Skillman Avenue and I'd cried when she turned to go. "Don't leave me here!" my five-year-old self had begged her. Now I was fifteen, but apparently my attitude toward going to a new school hadn't changed much.

"I really think home schooling sounds like a good idea," I told Sam.

She wiped the sweat off her forehead. "Unfortunately, reading *InStyle* cover to cover and watching marathons of *Trading Spaces* and *A Makeover Story* doesn't give you a good education." She fiddled with the broken air-conditioning knob, as if sheer desire might miraculously bring it to life. "You're lucky to be going back to school," she said. "I wish I was."

Sam was supposed to be starting college, but our lives had become sort of complicated since our father died suddenly of a heart attack in July. Actually, you could probably trace the whole thing back even further, to when our dad had married Enid Gutmyre. Enid, who looked like a Popsicle stick with red fingernails and a balloon-size head, considered children to be a notch below mosquitoes on the evolutionary scale. Her idea of a compliment was "Nose jobs would make you girls so pretty." Our mother had died six years earlier, so after our dad died Enid stood to become our legal guardian, and inherit everything. Enid's plan was to ship me off to a boarding school in the Canadian wilderness, where I'd never be heard from again.

To avoid that fate, my sister managed to divert our dad's money into her own account, and, with the help of her best friend Felix in Queens, and his mentor, Tony Difriggio—a major figure in the Midwestern criminal underworld—we'd secured fake identities, left New York in the middle of the night, and driven across the country. In the process, Sam had gone from being seventeen to twenty-one, and had become my legal (well, not exactly "legal"—Difriggio had printed official papers declaring her to be legal) guardian.

Unfortunately I was still stuck at fifteen.

I sighed and slung my bookbag over my shoulder. "It was not a good idea to stay up last night watching *Carrie*."

10

"Venice High will be bubble gum and peaches compared to that. Just try not to burn down the school or anything," she said.

"Thanks for the advice."

I smoothed out my skirt and got ready to face Venice High. Sam and I'd gone shopping at the Gondolier Mall on Saturday for an outfit for my first day of school and some work clothes for her. I'd bought a black sleeveless shirt, black miniskirt, and new black sandals. I opened the passenger door just as Noelle McBride's new pink Cadillac pulled into the empty parking space next to us.

"Did you just come from a funeral?" Noelle's best friend Lacey Lanning asked me as she stepped out of Noelle's car, eyeing my outfit.

I rolled my eyes. Couldn't they come up with a creative insult? Noelle's crowd was always harping on my all-black wardrobe. People in Venice rarely wore black unless they were off joining a convent or were in mourning; they wore pastels—mostly pink, yellow, and green. Maybe they felt they had to blend in with the corn and sunsets. I still hadn't adapted my wardrobe—I guess it's true what they say about taking the girl out of Queens. In New York, everyone wore black. Maybe we felt we had to blend in with the dirt.

Noelle and her friends Tara and Claire climbed out of her car and stood next to Lacey. All four of them wore matching yellow T-shirts and cropped pink pants. I suppressed an urge to make a citizen's arrest for fashion crimes.

"Noelle seems back to her old self," Sam said. This was pretty remarkable considering the tumultuous events of the summer—while attempting to pursue her dream of becoming a country music star (although her singing voice resembled a car engine in need of a tune-up) Noelle had been abducted by a record producer who had a few mental health issues, to put it mildly. When I got blamed for her disappearance, Sam and I, along with our friend Colin, figured out the whole thing and rescued her, clearing my name. For a little while afterward, Noelle had stopped insulting me directly and addressed me with saccharine sweetness. Now she just smiled a painfully wide grin and waved hello at us.

"Good luck," Sam told me. "You're gonna need it."

I hugged her, shut the car door, and watched longingly as she drove off in a puff of exhaust. Our car was Paleolithic, but it was the best untraceable car that Felix could get for us. Under Sam's urging, I'd signed up for mechanics class, so I'd have an inkling of insight into our car's near-weekly breakdowns. I hadn't put up much of a fight—I figured there would be some cute guys in the class.

I clunked up the steps in my new sandals and into the crowd thronging toward the school doors. I'd never seen so many unfamiliar faces in my life. Where did all these kids come from? I knew Venice High drew students from all the surrounding smaller towns, but I hadn't exr ˙ this many strangers.

 still in New York City, I would have been on
 7 train to my old school, the LaGuardia
 f Music & the Arts, with my best friend
 ˙h-braid my hair during the ride, and
 ˙ries from the cart on the corner near

12

Columbus Circle and eat them by the fountain at Lincoln Center. We'd meet up with our other friends, Julien, Dika, and Elizabeth, and head to school together. Instead, here I was in Indiana, all alone, and none of my old friends had any idea what had happened to me.

I wished Colin was here. He was our closest friend in town, and a junior at Venice High. He'd been in London visiting his dad for a few days, and he wasn't due back until that night.

The front entrance to Venice High featured a bronze statue of a muscular farmer leaning on a pitchfork and staring hopefully at the horizon. Beneath the farmer's feet a plaque read:

"The Crossroads of America"
INDIANA STATE MOTTO
Adopted 1937

Oy vay. I wished there was a subway stop I could dive into with a direct route to Queens.

Security was incredibly lax at Venice High—there were none of the ID cards, guards, or metal detectors that we had at LaGuardia. I moved with the throng through the front doors, down the air-conditioned lime green corridors, and then followed the signs to the registrar's office. I let out a breath I didn't know I was holding when I saw Fern—finally, a friendly face. Fern spent summers working in the front office at the Rose Country Club, the same place where Sam and I'd gotten jobs when we arrived in Venice. The rest of the year she

13

worked in the administration office at Venice High.

"Sophie—your big day! I got everything ready for you—course schedule, your records, everything's on file. I've been telling the whole office about you and your sister." She introduced me to the other women who worked there—Dotty, Lulu, and the principal, Mrs. Philbert. "We're so lucky to have you here at Venice High, you're bringing up the grade-point average of the whole sophomore class," Fern said.

I smiled, but felt a stab of guilt. Difriggio, our contact in Indianapolis, who'd given us new birth certificates and Social Security cards, had also created new school records for me. He'd upped my GPA from a 3.1 to a 3.9. It was pretty amazing to think about all the grades I'd labored and even cried over. That C in Sequential Math 1. I'd thought my dad was going to kill me for that grade and—poof!—now it was gone.

"Here you go." Fern handed me my schedule on an orange piece of paper. "First period English, second math, third biology, then lunch, mechanics, gym, and music. And you're not going to believe who your mechanics teacher is."

"Who?"

"Well, Rusty McMailer, who usually teaches it, dislocated his shoulder at the pig-wrestling competition, so Mrs. Philbert went and asked Chester."

"Really? Chester?" Things were looking up. Chester Jones was the first person we'd met in Venice; he was the local mechanic who'd spent countless hours fixing our car. He'd taken a liking to me and Sam.

I made my way toward my English class, and found a

seat in front. Tara, Noelle, Lacey, and Claire sat in a row in the back. To my right, a tall, pretty girl with long black hair read *Pride and Prejudice* at her desk. I loved that book. She wore a black T-shirt with the words VENICE ARTISTS' GUILD on it, along with a denim miniskirt and black sandals that looked a little like mine. I eyed the sandals—I had a theory that you could identify a potential kindred spirit just by her shoes.

I turned toward her. "Hey," I said. "What's the Venice Artists' Guild?"

She looked up and smiled. "It's an organization my mom started with other artists in the area. They want to revitalize Venice and have real art instead of the cheesy gondolier sculptures around town."

"Oh cool," I said. Although Venice intended to model itself after its Italian namesake, the town only had one canal and it was bone-dry and strewn with garbage and stray cats. While staring into the canal sometimes brought back fond memories of parts of Queens, the town was having trouble living up to its "Europe of the Midwest" slogan. I'd never been to Europe, but I had a feeling that the biggest tourist attraction in Venice, Italy, wasn't the chicken-fried steak.

The black-haired girl put her book away. "I'm Mackenzie," she said. "What's your name?"

"Sophie."

"You're new here, aren't you?" she asked.

I nodded. "My sister and I moved here from Cleveland in July."

That was our story: as far as everyone in Venice was concerned, Samantha and Sophia Shattenberg of Queens

15

never existed. Instead, Sam and Fiona Scott of Cleveland had arrived in town after a car accident had killed their parents. (Felix decided we had to change at least one of our names, since he didn't want two sisters listed on the books anywhere as Samantha and Sophia, and he'd always had a fondness for the name Fiona.) Lucky me. I had to tell people that Sophie was my nickname.

The bell rang, interrupting us. Mr. Nichols, the teacher, took attendance and scrawled the word HERITAGE across the blackboard. Then he read a poem titled "Heritage" by the African-American writer Countee Cullen. It was about missing your homeland, where your ancestors are from, even if you've never been there yourself.

"What do you think about this subject, heritage?" Mr. Nichols asked as he sat on the corner of his desk.

Everyone gaped at him like a convention of zombies.

"Mackenzie?" he asked.

She shifted in her seat, and her ears reddened. "Well, I guess for me...well, my family's part Native American. We're Hunkpapa Sioux from the Standing Rock Indian Reservation in South Dakota. . . . But I've never been there, so I guess I can understand what the poem's talking about. Sometimes I feel pretty removed from my ancestors, too."

"Good, good," Mr. Nichols said. "Anyone else?"

Everyone seemed suddenly preoccupied with the corn growing outside the window.

I could feel his eyes on me. Why had I sat in the front row? What had I been thinking?

He glanced at a paper on his desk, and then back at

me. "Fiona?" he asked.

"Um, people call me Sophie," I said. I could feel my face flush. I wanted to say that I was Jewish, that my dad had been born in Poland and he and his parents had escaped the Holocaust. My sister and I'd never been to Poland—we hardly knew anything about it. I was certainly removed from my ancestors and my heritage, too. But I couldn't say any of this out loud because I was supposedly Christian, from Cleveland.

I struggled to come up with something to say. "I guess, I mean in general, even if you've never been to the place where your people are from, you probably still have some sort of connection to it, to your heritage, I guess . . . or at least it probably makes your feelings about your heritage sort of complicated."

I wanted to sink under my chair, but Mr. Nichols nodded, smiling. "That's a good point."

I sighed, relieved, and made a mental note to talk to Sam about the "heritage" of the Scott family. We'd come up with a story about our parents, but hadn't gone back any further than that. We'd have to invent some Midwestern grandparents for ourselves pronto.

Mr. Nichols got up from the corner of his desk and passed out a sheet of paper that listed class expectations for the year. We were going to read *Huckleberry Finn*, *Macbeth*, *Their Eyes Were Watching God*, and short stories in a book called *Contemporary Literature*. The redheaded boy sitting next to me yawned at the prospect of these books, but I couldn't wait to read them. I liked Mr. Nichols. He seemed eager and enthusiastic, and about a hundred years younger than my English teacher at LaGuardia.

I had always loved books. Our house in Queens had been filled with them, from floor to ceiling in the living room, dining room, and hallways. I missed all those books, my parents' books. I used to love picking one off the shelves, sitting on the living-room couch, and devouring the whole thing on a Sunday afternoon. Now I did that at our friend Colin's shop. He and his father owned a store called Wright Bicycles, Etc., which was heavy on the "Etc."—in addition to used bikes, he sold antique furniture, tchotchkes, pottery, gargoyles, pocket watches, and shelves and shelves of used books. Sometimes I'd sit on his comfortable sofas and read all afternoon. I couldn't wait for him to get back in town.

When the bell rang, Mackenzie leaned over and asked what I had next.

I looked at my schedule. "Math, biology, lunch . . . "

"Fourth period? I've got lunch then, too. I'll look for you," she said.

"Okay." I smiled. I was relieved to have someone to sit with at lunch. Mackenzie seemed cool and interesting. Sam was always bugging me about how I could read intelligent books and then buy *Lucky* magazine—as if it was impossible to have a brain and also love makeup and clothes. From Mackenzie's outfit and her pale pink eye shadow, it seemed like she understood that the two could go together.

The bell rang for second period; we said good-bye, and I somehow made it through math and biology without falling asleep. Then it was time for lunch.

I walked into the school cafeteria, but I didn't see

18

Mackenzie anywhere. My heart began to pound. Entering a new school lunchroom was one of the most intimidating situations in life, I was sure. More intimidating than climbing Mount Everest or trekking across the Antarctic. I decided to get on the cafeteria line instead of standing in the middle of the room. My stomach sank when I saw the man behind the lunch counter—it was my old boss Henry. Henry had fired me for showing up late for work at the Rose Club concession stand and flirting with the club's lifeguard (who was also Noelle's ex-boyfriend), Troy Howard. Henry had since forgiven me, but he was never exactly a ray of sunshine.

"Hello, Fiona," he said. Even though I'd told him a million times to call me Sophie, he never seemed to get that straight.

"Hi, Henry."

His white apron was stained with ketchup. He gripped a large ladle with his hairy fingers. "What'll it be? We've got potato glop, pea goo, mystery meat, and mayo sandwiches with a little bit of tuna."

"I see you're in a cheery mood as usual," I said.

"Fiona, it's hotter than a pig on a spit back here. I'm sweating a river and it's not even noon." He stared at my outfit. "Still dressing like an undertaker, I see."

"Thanks, Henry. I'll have the mayo sandwich please."

He put the sandwich on my tray and I turned to scan the cafeteria. Where was Mackenzie? I squinted out the window. The cafeteria opened onto a lawn with picnic tables. Groups of students picnicked everywhere, despite the heat. Several girls sunbathed in halter tops; a group of

19

guys sprayed one another with water guns.

At one of the picnic tables I saw Noelle and her crowd. Colin's friends Fred and Larry were hanging out by the edge of the lawn, but I didn't know them very well. I didn't know where to go. I clutched my tray tightly; sweat formed under my palms.

Then someone tapped me on the shoulder. I turned and sagged with relief. It was Mackenzie.

"Sorry," she said. "Mr. Spector kept us late in chemistry. He's half-deaf and wouldn't believe us when we told him the bell rang. Want to sit by the Old Tree?"

"Sure!"

We walked outside to a weeping willow tree, its branches dipping to the ground, and sat in its shade. Mackenzie unpacked her lunch—a goat-cheese-and-apple sandwich with two slices of blueberry cake for dessert. She took one look at my tray and gave me half her sandwich and a whole piece of cake.

"Were you around this summer?" I asked her. I wished that she'd been hanging out at the pool...maybe then I would've had someone to talk to.

"My mom and I were away. She had a residency at an artists' community in Russia, and I went with her."

"Russia, really?" Considering that Indiana was the farthest my sister and I'd ever traveled, Russia sounded like another planet.

"A far cry from Venice, that's for sure," Mackenzie said. "It's good to be back, but Venice High is a weird place."

"Yeah. It's really different from my old school." I stared at my lunch tray. Hopefully she wouldn't ask

20

too much about it.

"I bet it's a huge change from Cleveland. We have so many cliques here," she said, shaking her head.

"Like what?"

"Well there's the ag clique—farmers' kids wearing flannel shirts and jeans and overalls even though it's ninety degrees. And over there, you've got the jocks and cheerleaders—my brother hangs out with them, he's on the football team." She rolled her eyes at the words *football team*.

As I looked over, I noticed that Noelle and her friends were part of that crowd, too. Troy, the lifeguard from the country club, sat beside them—apparently he and Noelle were friends again.

I felt awkward looking at Troy—I couldn't believe I'd been so in love with him over the summer, before I finally accepted that he had the brains of a fruit fly. I'd even gone on a date with him (well, sort of a date—the purpose of it was to find out information that would help us find Noelle). But half an hour after he dropped me off at home, Sam and I caught him making out with another girl at the drive-in.

"Then you've got the nerds, and then the punk and goth kids," Mackenzie continued, gesturing at the groups. "There are the faculty kids—children of professors from Wilshire College, that small liberal arts school two towns over." Colin's friends Fred and Larry were hanging out with those kids.

"So what's your crowd, then?" I asked her.

"I'm friends with some of the ags—my parents have a farm, about fifteen miles out of town—and the faculty kids, who are more into the arts than most people around here, but I don't know...I guess I don't really have one crowd. All the groups here are sort of...you know. Groups. Sometimes I just wish I was growing up in a big city. I'm planning to go to college in New York."

"Really?" I smiled. If only I could tell her that was where I was from.

"I want to go to NYU, or maybe to an art school, like Pratt."

I nodded, pretending I didn't know anything about those schools at all. My sister was supposed to be starting NYU, although according to our new identities she'd already graduated from college.

I wished I could tell Mackenzie about LaGuardia. I picked a blade of grass and rubbed it between my fingers. I missed my old school. I'd really been looking forward to all the courses I was going to take in the vocal program—opera and musical theater workshops, and Italian, German, and French vocal literature. I missed the state-of-the-art concert hall and recording studio, and the fact that the seniors got to give concerts at Carnegie Hall. Somehow, performing karaoke at the Rose Country Club for the next three years just didn't seem like much of a substitute.

Mackenzie took out a compact and applied a coat of lip gloss—MAC Lipglass, I had the same kind—then looked at her watch. "What do you have next?"

"Mechanics," I said.

"I took that last year. It's a good class," she said. "I learned how to install new brakes on my mom's truck."

I was liking Mackenzie more every minute—she

wore lip gloss and knew how to fix a car. She showed me her class schedule, to see if we had any other classes together. We did—seventh-period music.

"Great—I'll see you then," she said. We walked through the cafeteria and toward the main hall, where the bulletin boards were filled with flyers announcing all sorts of clubs and events and sign-up sheets—Chess Club, Drama Club, 4-H Fair, Bible Study, Rose Society Meeting, Sadie Hawkins Dance, Winslow Chamber Music Concert. Then a pink flyer caught my eye, and my heart leaped into my throat.

WILSHIRE COLLEGE HILLEL SOCIETY
AND THE DEPARTMENT OF ART HISTORY
PRESENT
Professor Leo Shattenberg
"Ivan Sebrid: Story of an Artist"
A Lecture
Jewish Cultural Center
Eight Wilshire Way
8:00 P.M. Friday, September 12

I ripped it off the board, my hand shaking.

"What's that?" Mackenzie asked.

"Um—a lecture—"

She studied the flyer. "Ivan Sebrid? I saw one of his paintings this summer. He's amazing," she said.

I'd heard of Ivan Sebrid—I vaguely remembered seeing ads for an exhibit of his work at the Jewish Museum in New York. My heart raced so fast I could barely breathe. Our real name, Shattenberg, was not a common name—I'd never met another Shattenberg before. Leo Shattenberg was the name of one of our relatives, who had supposedly died over fifty years ago, during the war.

"You're staring at that flyer as if it says you won a million dollars," Mackenzie said.

I struggled to get my heart back into my chest. "It—it looks like an interesting lecture," I stammered, trying to sound casual. This was better than a million dollars. All I could think was that I might have just found our only living relative in the world.

2

"Are you okay?" Mackenzie asked me. Students swarmed down the hall, heading to class, their knapsacks covering their backs like brightly colored shells.

I nodded. "I'm fine. I think I've just got first-day jitters. We better get to class. I'll see you in music." We said good-bye, and after she was out of sight I headed straight for the pay phones in the basement.

I quickly dialed Sam's number at work; she was the full-time assistant for Gus Jenkins, private detective. She picked up after one ring. "Jenkins and Associates."

"You're not going to believe what I just found," I whispered into the phone.

"Don't tell me. Lip gloss that stays on all day."

"I'm serious." I took the flyer from my pocket and unfolded it. "It's an announcement—I found it tacked to the wall at school. There's some professor giving a lecture about the artist Ivan Sebrid—"

"That's what's so important?"

"It's the professor's name. It's Leo—" I lowered my voice even more, and lingered on every syllable—

25

"Shattenberg."

I heard a muffled clanking noise.

"Sorry," she said. "I dropped the phone."

"I'm sure it's him," I said. "It has to be."

"Where are you?" Sam asked.

"At school. In the basement."

"No one can hear you, right?"

I glanced down the empty hall. "Nobody's here."

"I want to see it," she said. "I'm coming right over."

"I have class now. I'm supposed to be in mechanics, with Chester."

"Tell Chester you're not feeling well—he'll understand. I'll meet you out front in five minutes."

"Okay." I put the receiver back. My hand was still trembling.

Leo Shattenberg. Two years ago, when I was in eighth grade at J.H.S. 125, my social studies teacher, Mr. Mankewitz, had assigned us a project to chart our family trees, including biographical notes about our relatives. This wasn't easy to do—both my parents were from Jewish immigrant families who'd narrowly escaped the Holocaust, and only my parents and three grandparents had survived. All my grandparents, and my mother, had died by the time of the assignment, so my dad was the only one I could talk to. His information was sketchy. He could barely remember all the names of his own relatives.

"My great-uncle Hymie, the potato farmer . . . or was it Heschel?" he'd mused. "Married to Gittel, or no, I think it was Irena. Or Rose?"

"You don't remember your own family?" I'd asked.

26

My dad shrugged. "What do I know of these cousins? I was a baby when we left Europe. They died before I could know them."

He knew the places of death of some relatives, because the Red Cross had notified his parents. But others he wasn't sure of. For several relatives, he wasn't even sure if they'd died at all. One of these was Leo Shattenberg, my grandfather's first cousin. My dad knew that Leo's parents had died in the concentration camp Bergen-Belsen, but official word of Leo's death had never come.

"It was like that for a lot of people during the war," my dad explained. "A lot of people were missing, with no proof that they died. Jews were shot in mass graves during the war. Some tried to escape and were found and shot in the woods with no witnesses. Anything could have happened."

I'd searched for Leo on the Internet but nothing had come up. I'd taken it for granted that he'd died. On the family tree, I'd scribbled Leo's name and written "presumed dead."

But maybe that was wrong. Maybe he was alive.

How many Leo Shattenbergs could there be in the world? I'd thought—I'd been certain—that Sam and I were the only family we had. Some of my friends in New York had five brothers and sisters and endless aunts, uncles, cousins . . . it seemed almost incomprehensible that it was just Sam and me. One night a couple weeks ago I'd dreamed that our house was full of relatives, aunts and uncles and cousins, filling the living room, chatting, cooking food. In real life I'd have settled for just one more relative—for Leo being alive.

I rushed to the mechanics classroom and tapped on the door. Chester opened it, and twenty faces gazed at me. Even with the shock of finding the flyer, my brain still registered the fact that there were more cute guys inside than I'd ever seen in my life. Actually—the class was all guys. There was one, standing near the door, who was so handsome I couldn't help but stare at him.

I tried to focus on Chester. "I'm not feeling well . . . I was wondering if you would mind if I went to the nurse this period, to lie down?"

He felt my forehead and peered at me through his bifocals. "You do feel warm," he said. He stuck his hands back in his overall pockets. "You go to the nurse's right now. Don't worry about class."

I scurried down the hall, and out the main doors. Sam was already outside, in the Buick.

"Get inside," she said. "Where is it?"

"Right here." I handed the flyer to her. She steered out of the parking lot. "Where are we going?" I asked.

"I just want to drive somewhere private and look at it." Her forehead shone with sweat. She glanced at the flyer while she drove past the lawn and football field, through the cornfields and farmland surrounding the campus. "I can't believe this was just hanging up at your school."

"It's got to be him," I said.

"Let's not get too excited about it yet," she said, but her voice wavered. We turned down a deserted dirt road that cut through a pasture. "I mean, what are the chances we'd have some relative here, in Indiana?"

"Well, what are the chances that we'd be here in Indiana?" We had to stop the car as a brown cow tramped across the road. "Maybe it's some weird kind of fate thing," I said. "Maybe this is somehow meant to be. We were meant to find him."

Sam usually brushed off my notions of fate and co-incidence, saying my head was in the clouds and I watched too many romantic comedies. But this time she didn't say anything.

After the cow passed by we drove a little farther, and she parked the car. "Let's get out and walk. I want to stretch my legs," she said.

The sun beat down on us. My sandals got dusty as we walked down the road.

"What do we know about Leo Shattenberg?" she asked. "We know he was born in Poland, and that branch of the family moved to Vienna, right? I thought they were all killed, though, that no one from that part of the family survived."

"Daddy assumed Leo died with the rest of his family, but he wasn't certain about it. Leo was officially miss-ing. Notification about his death never came."

"But if Leo did survive, then why didn't he contact the rest of the family?" she asked. "Why didn't he con-tact us, or Daddy, or Bubbe and Zayde, a long time ago? It just doesn't make sense that he wouldn't have tried to get in touch with us. If he's our relative, we should already know about him."

I picked a wildflower off the side of the road. "Maybe he tried to find us but couldn't," I said. "Maybe he was too broken up over the loss of all his other relatives and didn't want to get in touch. Maybe—maybe he had amnesia after the war and only remembered his name later on—"

"You're beginning to sound like a Lifetime Original Movie. Next you're going to say he has an evil twin."

"Maybe he does," I said. "Who knows? I think we should just go to the lecture, meet him, and find out for ourselves."

"But how are we going to find out? We can't just say, 'Um, excuse me, Mr. Shattenberg? Our official names are Sam and Fiona Scott, although actually we're really Samantha and Sophia Shattenberg of Queens. We're orphaned criminals using fake identities and lucky you, we think we're related'?!"

"We can be a little more subtle," I said.

We walked on; the pasture seemed to stretch on forever. Sam glanced at her watch. "I should take you back. We can talk about this more after school. In the meantime I'll go see if I can find out anything about Leo on the Internet. How's your first day going, by the way?"

"It's looking up. I like my English teacher, and I met a really cool girl named Mackenzie. And in mechanics I'm the only girl in the class."

She narrowed her eyes at me. "I guess this means you'll be getting an A in mechanics."

"An A-plus." I wiped dirt off my new shoes. "How's work?"

"Finding Noelle was a piece of cake compared to finding the floor of Gus's office," she said. Gus Jenkins had hired Sam and me as assistants at his detective agency after we'd rescued Noelle McBride; I was going

30

to help out after school and on weekends. His office was in an old factory building next to Muther's, his favorite bar, and it was the messiest place I'd ever seen in my life. It resembled a Salvation Army drop-off center, with piles of clothes, books, papers, Styrofoam cups, file boxes, and even a couple of random broken appliances strewn about.

"How's the cleanup coming?"

Sam shook her head. "I found a ham sandwich in his closet that looked like it was from 1970."

"Ewww." I scrunched up my nose.

Sam locked her arm in mine as we made our way back to the car. "I hope it's him," she said.

"Me, too."

She dropped me at school. "I'll see you at home later—I'll come back early," she said, and sped off.

I somehow survived gym class, despite a violent episode of volleyball in which I spent the whole class running for my life every time someone yelled "Spike!" Finally, at long last, it was time for music.

I found a seat and saved the one next to me for Mackenzie. Our music books were already set out on each desk in front of us. *A Celebration of American Music.* I opened the table of contents. Uh-oh. Not looking good. I stared at the titles: "Magic Penny," "You Are My Sunshine," "All God's Critters."

Mackenzie sat down next to me and put her black bookbag on the floor.

"Look at these songs," I said.

"I know," she said. "Mrs. Oderkirk isn't exactly into

contemporary music, to say the least. We're not going to be singing any Evil Barbie songs, that's for sure."

"You know Evil Barbie?" They were a band from New York that not many people had heard of.

"I love them," she said. "I've been trying to play some of their stuff on my violin, but it's not going so well."

"I play guitar," I said. "I know a couple of their songs."

"You should come over sometime. We'll play together. I'm not great, but I'm learning."

"I'd love to." I nodded, excited to have someone to play music with again.

Mrs. Oderkirk began the class by plugging in her electric keyboard. Unfortunately E-flat was malfunctioning; every time she pressed it, it moaned like a wounded donkey. Mackenzie and I tried not to laugh.

Mackenzie scribbled in her notebook: *What are you doing next Friday before the lecture?*

The lecture? I wrote.

"The Ivan Sebrid flyer you ripped off the wall?" she whispered. "You're going, right? I was thinking about it, and I'd like to go, too. Maybe you can come over after school, and then we'll go to the lecture together. You can see our farm—we've got sheep, goats, pigs, chickens, and a cow. It's kind of a hobby farm—my dad's also a doctor in Winslow. But it's pretty."

The closest I'd ever been to a farm were the pigs at the Central Park Zoo. I wanted to see Mackenzie's place and spend time with her and play music, but I thought Sam would kill me if Mackenzie came to the lecture, too.

"Oh. I should probably check with my sister . . .

32

sometimes we do stuff on Friday afternoons."

"Okay." She looked a little hurt.

I felt bad—I wanted to spend time with her. I'd been missing Viv so much and I felt the same kind of connection with Mackenzie, the rush of liking the same things and the feeling like we'd known each other for much longer. It seemed more important to spend time with her than to worry about what might happen if she attended the lecture with us. "Actually, I'd love to see your farm. We can meet up with my sister afterward and all go to the lecture together," I said.

"You sure?" she asked.

I nodded. "It'd be fun."

Mrs. Oderkirk barked at us to stop talking in class. I sank in my seat, my insides knotted with thoughts of how I'd tell Sam that Mackenzie was coming, too. How would I explain this one?

I took the bus home from school, sitting right behind Ethel, the driver, in her pink shirt and pink sunglasses. Ethel also drove the public Rose-Tran bus around town.

Ethel got on the microphone. "I've got an announcement for all riders of Venice Public Transportation. All Rose-Tran service will be suspended the next three Friday evenings, due to a special situation."

"What's going on?" I asked.

She turned off the microphone and glanced at me in the rearview mirror. "I won the raffle at the chamber-of-commerce booth at the Rose Festival. I'm getting a free series of—what do you call it? Defoliation treatments, at the Venice Beauty Palace."

I pictured Ethel getting leaves plucked from all over her body. "You mean exfoliation?" I asked.

"That's right. With fruit acids or something. Sounds a little frightening if you ask me."

"Fruit acids are good," I said.

"Well, hopefully when it's done I'll look your age again."

"Probably," I said. Ethel was in her sixties. These sorts of conversations never seemed to happen with the bus drivers in Queens.

Ethel dropped me off in front of our house, a pink Victorian cottage with a front porch and two floors, just a couple blocks from the dry canal. Sam came home a half-hour after me and plopped down on our couch. "I Googled Leo, but nothing came up. No former addresses, nothing."

She reached into her bag and pulled out a pad of personalized stationery she'd had made—JENKINS DETECTIVE AGENCY, it read. In smaller print it said *Gus Jenkins, Detective. Sam Scott, Sophie Scott, Assistants.*

"Wow, it looks so official," I said.

"Yeah. Now all we need are some cases. Gus went home today to try to find his file of contacts so we can drum up some business. Three hours later I called him— he found the file, after digging under his bed all afternoon. It had been compiled by his former secretary, a Russian woman named Svetlana, when he was on the Chicago police force."

"You must be glad he found it."

"Yeah. Except the whole file is written in Russian," Sam said.

"Ooh. Not good."

She went into the kitchen and opened a can of Yoo-Hoo, her ultimate comfort food. "All afternoon I've been trying to remember what Daddy told us about Leo," Sam said, "but I just can't. Do you still have that project you did for school—the family tree?"

I shook my head. I'd left it behind with so much of our other stuff when we'd fled Queens. It still bothered me how many things we hadn't taken. I wished we'd been able to keep more, but we'd only had room for whatever we could cram in the car.

"You must remember something."

I stared up at the ceiling. "Daddy said that Zayde had talked about Leo a lot . . . Leo was one of his favorite cousins. He said that Leo collected butterflies . . . and he was crazy about chocolate." I remembered drawing a picture of a butterfly and a Hershey bar, among other random objects, on the cover of my school project. I'd thought illustrations might distract Mr. Mankewitz from the vague information inside.

"Great. Butterflies and chocolate. That only describes about ten million kids in the world," she said.

"He also said Leo loved bicycling—he even talked about biking around the world someday."

"Butterflies, chocolate, and bicycling. That's almost as definitive as a DNA test." She let out a long sigh, and started making notes on the pad.

> *Leo Shattenberg: Identifying Details*
> *Loves chocolate*
> *Collects butterflies*

Born in Poland between 1920–1930
Loves to ride his bicycle

"Also, if he's our Leo, then he should know the names of our other cousins," she said. She added:

Has relatives named Heschel, Gertrude,
David, and Solomon

We stared at our paltry list.

"Well, it's a start," I said.

"I just get the feeling that there were lots of people in Poland at that time named Leo, and probably just as many Heschels, Gertrudes, Davids, and Solomons. It's not like any of our relatives had rare Hebrew names like Shlimey or something," she said.

One of our neighbors in Queens had married a man named Shlimey, from Israel. "I'm glad we don't have any Shlimey Shattenbergs on our family tree. Though Heschel doesn't sound exactly common to me. How many Heschels do you know?"

"We're talking about Poland in the 1920s and '30s. I bet there were a gazillion Heschels. And what are we going to ask him? 'Are you perchance related to any Heschels? And what are your feelings on chocolate?'"

"We'll find a way," I said.

"Pelt him with Godivas and see how he reacts?"

"We can work it into the conversation," I said.

"How are you going to do that? It's a lecture about art. 'Thank you for that point about post-impressionism, but could you please tell me how you feel about truffles?'"

36

"We'll ask him questions about his lecture, and bring it up naturally," I said.

"Okay. If you say so."

I could hear the skepticism in her voice. I knew I needed to tell her about Mackenzie coming, too, but it didn't seem like a good time to bring it up.

She tapped her pen against the table. "We also need to find out more about Ivan Sebrid, to make our interest in the lecture seem natural."

"I bet Colin has a book on him," I said. "He's got that whole huge bookshelf of art history books. I'm sure there's something on Sebrid."

She glanced at her watch. "I wonder if he's back yet—he was supposed to be home sometime tonight."

"Let's go see," I said, feeling a chill of excitement. Colin was one of the few people in Venice who I felt we could trust no matter what. When the Venice police caught me driving without a license, Colin was the person I'd turned to, and he'd comforted me and helped me get out of a sticky situation. I'd missed him more than I'd realized, and now I couldn't wait to see him.

Wright Bicycles, Etc, was in a yellow house just a few blocks away from ours. I quickened my pace when I saw the light glowing inside—Colin was home.

He answered the door right away. The shop was filled with empty suitcases and boxes only partially unpacked. His brown bangs fell into his eyes as he hugged Sam, and then me.

"I was just about to call you guys," he said. "I got back a half-hour ago."

"We missed you," I said into his hair while he wrapped his arms around me. He'd only been gone a few days but he looked different. He wore a button-down shirt instead of his usual paint-spattered clothing.

"You look nice. Did you meet some British chick or something?" Sam asked him, her hand on her hip.

"Nah," he said, grinning. "My dad just thought I should have some 'proper clothing.'"

"Where is your dad?" Sam asked. "I thought he was coming back with you."

Colin walked over to one of his boxes. "Yeah, we'd planned to fly back together, but he got detained on a new case." Colin's dad was an incredibly busy international business lawyer—he traveled the world so much, he was barely ever home. Colin's mother had died three years ago, of cancer; I'd sort of begun to think of Colin as an orphan, too.

He pulled something out of the box. "These are for you," he said. He handed packages wrapped in green paper to Sam and me. Sam opened hers first.

It was an early hardcover edition of Charlotte Perkins Gilman's *Women and Economics*—a perfect gift for my sister, whose idea of fun was watching *Wall $treet Week* on PBS. "I love it," she said.

Then I opened mine: a red leather-bound journal.

"I know how you loved Anne Frank's diary and I thought you'd like one of your own to write in," he said.

"It's perfect." I kissed him on the cheek. He blushed.

"I also got something for both of you." He handed us a brown cardboard box.

"What is it?" I tore it open and pulled out a Sherlock

Holmes–style cap and dark wood pipe.

"I got them at the 221b Baker Street store in London," Colin said.

I put on the cap. "The game is afoot!" I said, Sherlock-style.

Sam pretended to smoke the pipe. "Confound you!"

Colin laughed. "Now what would I want with any British girls?"

"Obviously nothing," I said.

He brought us glasses of lemonade and filled us in on his trip. After he'd finished, Sam walked over to the end-less array of books lining the walls. "Hey, have you heard of the painter Ivan Sebrid?" she asked him.

Colin raised his eyebrows. "Yeah . . . Russian, Jewish, traveled across Europe in the early 1900s . . . " He scanned the shelves until his fingers rested on a huge book. "What did you want to know?"

"Sophie saw a flyer for a lecture about him at Wilshire College, and we thought we'd go . . . we've been thinking we could use a little culture. We wanted to read up on him first."

Colin took the book off the shelf and handed it to us. On the cover was a fanciful painting of a rural village in bright colors.

"When's the lecture?" he asked.

"Next Friday," Sam said.

"Oh good. We can all go together," he said.

Sam flipped through the book's pages noisily. "That's okay, you don't have to come," she told Colin.

"You don't want me to?"

"No, of course I want you to," she said. "But it's a

Friday night—I thought you'd want to do something more interesting."

"This is Venice. What's more interesting to do on a Friday night?"

"Lots of stuff," I said. "Cow-tipping, pig-wrestling, and riding the Rose-Tran bus around in circles. Oh wait—I forgot—there's no bus service next Friday—Ethel's exfoliating."

"What?" Sam asked. I told them about Ethel's beauty treatment.

Colin sank down in the couch next to me. "Now you see why I'm coming with you."

3

"Great," Sam said as we walked back home, lugging the Sebrid book. She shook her head. "There's no way we can ask Leo personal questions with Colin there, without sounding suspicious."

"Well . . . the thing is, Mackenzie's coming, too," I blurted out.

"What? Who?"

"Mackenzie, my new friend from school? She was there when I found the flyer. She's into Ivan Sebrid. She's even seen his paintings. She kind of invited herself, and well, I couldn't think of a way to un-invite her without sounding suspicious or mean."

Sam shook her head. "Why don't we just bring the whole town? Especially Police Chief Callowe and Officer Alby. I bet they'd love to come and hear all sorts of insinuating details about our secret identities."

"It'll be okay," I said. "Mackenzie and Colin don't know why we're really going."

We reached our front door; Sam unlocked it and we slouched on the living-room sofa.

"I guess we don't have a choice," she said. "But this is going to make it even harder to get information, you know."

"I know."

She sighed. "I've been thinking . . . this whole thing kind of puts us in a difficult situation, because even if Leo does turn out to be our relative, what good does it do us? We can't even tell him we're related."

My shoulders sank. "I guess not." Difriggio had given us an ironclad commandment that we couldn't tell a soul about our real identities. I doubted there was an exception for long-lost relatives emerging out of the blue.

I gazed at my stuffed polar bear Ed, resting on top of the bookcase. Ed had been one of the last things I'd grabbed when we left our house in Queens. It seemed like a strange force had brought us to Indiana, causing our car to break down in this little town. Not only was Indianapolis the home of our contact, Tony Difriggio, but it was where our mom had died, too. She'd disappeared on a business trip to Indianapolis, and it wasn't until two years later that she was confirmed dead, after a man confessed to her murder. Although her body was never found, they discovered DNA evidence that linked the murderer to the crime. She'd been gone for so long now, but I still missed her every single day. I wondered if the reason we'd ended up back in Indiana now was so that we could find Leo.

"It just seems like . . . this whole Leo thing is so odd, such a strange coincidence, that we don't even have a choice. We have to check it out. We'll just go to the lecture and see what we think. You know?" I said.

Sam gazed at me intently. "I want to make sure you're not getting your hopes up too much, though. I worry because you get carried away sometimes, and it may turn out that he's not our relative."

"Yeah, but maybe he is. And you want him to be, too." I wasn't ready to give up hope yet.

"Promise me you're not going to get all emotional when you meet him and erupt into some *Days of Our Lives* 'are you my relative?' weepy scene?"

"What do you take me for? I'm a complete professional. I helped find Noelle, didn't I? And anyway, I never watch *Days of Our Lives*. I watch *General Hospital*."

She gazed at the ceiling. "Why can't I have a normal sister?"

"I often ask myself the same thing," I said.

In English class the following Friday, Mr. Nichols told us to work in pairs and interview each other about our heritages.

"So tell me about your relatives," Mackenzie asked, her pen poised over her pink notebook.

"We're actually of Irish and Scottish descent," I said. My acting skills were getting better by the day. Sam and I'd discussed our fabricated family history in depth, so I was prepared for these questions.

"What were some of their names?"

We'd invented a whole new family tree. "Well, there's Great-Grandma Fiona Scott—that's who I'm named after. They came over from Scotland in 1894 and settled in

43

Ohio. Grandpa Scott worked in a textile business."

"Textiles." Mackenzie nodded, taking notes. "Where in Scotland were they from?"

"The Isle of Skye," I said. Sam and I'd seen that on the map and liked the way it sounded.

"You know I'm part Scottish, too," Mackenzie said. "I'm named after my paternal grandmother, who was born in Scotland . . . Esther Mackenzie from the Isle of Lewis."

"Wow," I said. I hoped Esther didn't know any Scotts from the Isle of Skye.

She told me more about her history—her mom had traced their lineage back six generations, from Medicine Bear to Ita ta win, which meant Wind Woman. Mackenzie's great-grandmother had been sent to government Indian schools to "re-educate the savage," as the government had put it. It was a pretty amazing history. I wished I could tell her who I really was.

After we finished interviewing each other she asked, "Can you still come over after school?"

I nodded. "I can't wait to see your farm. You know . . . I've actually never been on a farm before."

"You're kidding me." She gazed at me as if I'd said I'd never seen a TV.

"No—my friends in Cleveland all lived in the city."

After school she drove me out to her farm in her mom's blue pickup truck—she was lucky to already be sixteen, with full driving privileges. We rode past cornfields and meadows, horse pastures and cows grazing, to a long dirt driveway with a "Summerfield Farm" sign flapping in the breeze. Their farmhouse lay in the

44

distance, along with a barn and a silo. Horses grazed in their field.

"Horses," I said in awe, though it came out as *hawses*. I was still trying to get rid of my accent. I coughed, but Mackenzie didn't say anything.

"I can't believe you live here," I said. "It's so beautiful. It's like living in the middle of a *Little House on the Prairie* episode."

"I guess you could say that," she said, and laughed.

She parked the truck. I stared out at the fields and meadows, bright green against the blue horizon. Sam and I'd loved the *Little House on the Prairie* books when we were kids. We used to play a game based on it in the afternoons, alternating between who got to be Laura and who got to be Mary.

I wondered if Leo had a farm. Were there any Jewish farmers? I pictured my dad in overalls, tilling the land. "Oy, I'd love this if it weren't for my sciatica," he'd probably say.

"What's so funny?" Mackenzie asked.

"Oh—nothing. I was just thinking about Ethel at the beauty salon."

Mackenzie took me around to the back of the barn, to her mother's studio. We knocked on the door. "Mom," she said to a tall woman with a long mane of dark, wavy hair and green eyes. "This is Sophie—I told you about her, from English and music class? Sophie, this is my mom."

Mackenzie's mom wore a large men's shirt and was bent over a chunk of black stone. She was a sculptor, and the back of the barn was filled with all sorts of

45

strange-looking tools and materials, and hunks of rock and clay. She wiped off her hands and shook mine. "I'm Lynne," she said.

I smiled at her but could feel my throat tighten. Sometimes a part of me almost forgot that most kids our age had parents. My mom hadn't been an artist, but she'd managed an art gallery. I wished I could come home like Mackenzie and find my mom there, all warm and smiling. I felt like half of me was a normal teenager, worrying about boys and shoes and lip gloss, and the other half of me was so different from everybody else. That half of me had flashes of my parents, like now, in the middle of the day, every detail of them as clear as a photograph—I remembered exactly how my mom looked the last time I saw her. She'd been wearing a turquoise scarf, silver onyx earrings, a black cashmere sweater, a long maroon skirt, and brown suede boots with high heels. And I could still see my dad the night before he died, sitting at the kitchen table in his Mangy Mutt T-shirt, smearing a toasted sesame bagel with cream cheese.

"This is Sophie's first time seeing a farm," Mackenzie told her mom. "She's from Cleveland."

"Well, this is a pretty small farm," Lynne said. "I hope you like it."

Small? You could fit my entire Queens neighborhood in their cornfield. "I already love it," I said.

We went into the kitchen, where Mackenzie's brother Hayden and his friend sat at the table eating. Hayden's friend turned around and I almost jumped—it was the incredibly handsome guy from mechanics class. His

46

name was Pete Teagarden, I'd noted when Chester had taken attendance. I'd already scrawled *Pete Teagarden* repeatedly in the margins of my notebook.

I'd been too shy to say anything or even go near him, not to mention being intimidated by engines and carburetors and the whole greasy mess that was mechanics. But now he turned around and actually spoke to me.

"Hey," he said.

I almost passed out.

"You guys ate all the cookies, you creeps," Mackenzie said.

Hayden grabbed her and started tickling her. "Stop!" she screamed.

I felt so awkward around Pete. I wondered if there was a psychological term for Handsome-Guy-Turning-Your-Brains-to-Mush Complex. Severe clinical HGTBMC? I'd first shown signs of the syndrome when I'd met Troy over the summer; now I was catching it again with a vengeance.

"What do you think of mechanics class?" Pete asked.

"Oh, it's the greatest!" What was wrong with me? I decided to just keep my mouth shut.

Mackenzie struggled free from her brother. "Want some ice cream?" She got a pint of chocolate Häagen-Dazs out of the freezer, and two spoons. "I'm going to show Sophie the farm," she told her brother and Pete. "She's never been on one before."

Both Hayden and Pete raised their eyebrows at me.

We ate a few bites of ice cream, and then she led me outside. We walked back toward the barn, to a pen filled with goats and sheep. She warned me that the goats might bite, but I could pet the sheep. I ran my hand through the fur of a big fat one. It was soft, thick, and sort of greasy. "It's the lanolin," she explained.

To the left of the sheep pen was the chicken coop. Brown-and-white chickens waddled around, pecking up seed with their beaks. Some sat on their nests in wooden boxes along the wall. Mackenzie reached into one nest and pulled out a brown egg.

I'd never actually seen an egg fresh out of a chicken before. It was warm and smooth in my palm. She put it back in the nest, and we walked across the dirt road to the cornfield, and through the rows. "I used to love to run down the rows as a little kid," she said, marching briskly ahead.

As we left the cornfield and walked back toward the barn, Hayden and Pete joined us.

"So do you like the farm?" Pete asked.

"Oh, it's great," I said, trying hard not to say something dumb or embarrassing. Mackenzie wandered toward the field, chasing a stray cat. Out of the corner of my eye, I spotted a little lamb poking out from behind the barn. "Oh look—how cute," I said, walking toward it.

"Watch out," Hayden warned me. "That lamb has a problem—it might start chasing you. It bites."

"Really?"

"I'm serious," he said. "There's something wrong with it."

"Hayden has a scar from it," Pete said. Hayden showed me a mark on his leg.

"Oh my God," I said. I turned to catch up with Mackenzie, who was now in the field.

After I'd walked a few feet away, Hayden cried, "Look out!"

The lamb bounded toward me. I started running. The lamb ran faster.

"Watch out!" Hayden yelled. "Killer lamb!"

I ran quickly, but the lamb caught up and I screamed as loud as I could. Then I turned around and saw Hayden and Pete laughing so hard they looked like they were about to fall over.

Mackenzie jogged in my direction, shaking her head. "I'm sorry. I should've warned you. That numbskull over there called my brother thinks that's really funny." She rolled her eyes. "That's just hysterical, guys," she said to Hayden and Pete.

They were crouched by the fence, still laughing.

"It's a bottle lamb—it was orphaned, so it grew up with us feeding it, and it runs after people, wanting food. But it doesn't bite—it's harmless," Mackenzie said.

"Hmmph," I said, straightening my slightly rumpled clothes. "How was I supposed to know?"

When they finally recovered from their laughter, Pete put his hand on my shoulder. "That was pretty funny, Sophie."

I felt a little thrill as he touched me, but I was still mortified. "Great," I said. "Glad I could provide the entertainment."

I brushed off my pants. I doubted that Pete would ever be interested in me after witnessing that.

"Let's go up to my room," Mackenzie said. I followed her inside and upstairs. Her room was on the top floor of the house; it was painted a dark purple, with three

49

big windows and glow-in-the-dark stars on the ceiling. Outside I could see cornfields and horses grazing in the pasture, which rolled on for what seemed like forever. Mackenzie's cat was curled up on her bed in a little brown-and-black speckled ball of fur. "This is Yoda," Mackenzie said. She picked up the cat and cuddled it in her arms.

She reclined on the bed and I slid into a soft blue chair.

Mackenzie tilted her head. "Can I ask you something?"

My stomach turned over. What did she want to know? Had she heard that *hawses* slip? Was she suspicious of me not knowing anything about farm life? Did she guess that I was hiding something? "Sure," I said quietly.

"What happened to your parents?"

I stared at the woven rug on her floor. I breathed deeply; part of me was relieved that she hadn't guessed that my whole life was made up, but I hated answering this question. During our interviews with each other in English class I'd mentioned that my parents had died, but I hadn't explained it. She'd let the comment pass without asking more, until now.

"It was a car accident," I said. "This June." Our car-accident story had become second nature by now. In some ways the lie made it a little easier to talk about, because then I didn't have to think too much about what had really happened.

"That's so awful," Mackenzie said. "I don't know what I'd do . . . "

I hated thinking about how everyone I met from now

on would never know my parents. It just felt easier to put all those feelings away and ignore them altogether. I decided to change the subject; I looked at the clock. "We better get ready—we have to meet Sam and Colin soon."

We grabbed a quick dinner of sandwiches from the fridge, and then left for the lecture.

Wilshire College sat perched on a hill above fields, meadows, horse stables, and a forest. Quaint brick buildings and clapboard houses dotted the campus of the small liberal arts school, thirty miles from Venice.

We parked the car in a tiny lot and walked through the quad to the student center. Even at night the campus buzzed with students rushing around, laughing and talking. Music blared from dorm windows; we strolled through the student center, filled with flyers announcing Womyn's Springfest, Pink Triangles Week, Peace and Justice Week. Other signs announced lectures (I saw the Leo Shattenberg flyer again) and meetings for groups with mystifying acronyms—CISLA, LBGPU. Students wore tie-dyes and anklets with bells; others wore combat boots and had spiked hair, and we saw a few girls in pastels like most of the kids in Venice. Sam's shoulders sank as she took in the variety and energy of the scene—I could tell she wished she could be at NYU right now.

Colin and Mackenzie had been to the campus before, for concerts and events, but neither knew where the Hillel, the Jewish Cultural Center, was. We asked a student walking by, who pointed us in the direction of a pretty white house with green shutters.

Inside the house, my eyes focused on the mezuzah on the door, the Shabbos candles and antique menorahs in glass cabinets in the hall, and the Israeli folk art on the walls. It felt comfortable and familiar. In New York I'd never really thought about being Jewish. You didn't have to; being Jewish was in the air there, in everything—knishes on every corner and bagels in every deli, Yiddish words intermingled in people's speech. In some ways, leaving New York City and pretending we weren't Jewish had actually made me feel more Jewish than I'd ever felt before. I'd never realized how much I would miss it.

A crowd gathered in the large living room for the lecture. Chairs had been set up in front of a lectern. I scanned the room until my gaze settled on an older man with wisps of white hair covering his bald spot. He wore a tailored black suit and fiddled with several index cards in his hands.

Leo.

He looked to be in his late seventies—good sign—and when he smiled his eyes crinkled and his cheeks turned pink. I started to sweat. Despite what I'd told Sam, a part of me wanted to throw my arms around him, soap-opera-family-reunion style.

We took our seats, Mackenzie and Sam on either side of me and Colin next to Sam. Mackenzie studied the program, oblivious to the cloud of emotion brewing inside me. Sam read the program, too; she pointed a finger to the paragraph that stated Leo Shattenberg's biography—"Born in Poland, Dr. Shattenberg now lives in Bloomington, Indiana. He retired two years ago from his position as professor of art history at Indiana University." *Poland*. It had to be him. I squeezed my sister's hand and tried to appear casual.

A young, attractive guy stood up at the podium. He had dark brown hair and light blue eyes.

"Hi—thank you for coming. I'm Josh Shattenberg," he said. I squeezed Sam's hand again. Another Shattenberg? It suddenly occurred to me that the possibility of Leo being our relative also meant that his other relatives would be our relatives, too—we could have even more family we'd never known of. This guy Josh, standing before us, could be our cousin. Shattenbergs were multiplying like bunnies, right before our eyes.

"I'm a member of the Wilshire College Hillel society," Josh continued, "and I'm proud to introduce our guest lecturer tonight—my grandfather, Dr. Leo Shattenberg."

Dr. Shattenberg stepped to the podium. He spoke in a gentle, familiar voice with a faint, lilting Eastern European accent, like the way I remembered my grandfather Zayde speaking. He discussed the history of Ivan Sebrid—born in Russia to a poor Hasidic family, Sebrid studied in St. Petersburg and then moved to Paris and Vienna, where he developed his distinctive childlike, surreal style.

The lights dimmed and Leo showed slides of Sebrid's paintings. His bright-colored work featured animals, workmen, couples, musicians, and scenes of Jewish villages. Leo talked about how Sebrid's work showed the influence of the Cubists and Surrealists and then I zoned out from his lecture and started to daydream. I imagined going to Leo Shattenberg's for holidays: on Hanukkah Josh and I'd light the candles, sing "Mo'oz Tzur," eat latkes Leo had made (they'd be perfect, not too greasy and heavy, but just right, with heaps of applesauce and sour cream), and then we'd play Dreidl for M&M's. Leo and Josh would have us over for our birthdays, with homemade cakes. Leo and Josh and other as-yet-unknown-to-us cousins would come to my high school graduation, occupying entire rows of bleachers. I'd play guitar for them, show them my report cards; we'd take family vacations to Florida and the Grand Canyon, and Josh would help me with my college applications. I was imagining Leo walking me down the aisle at my wedding when before I knew it, everyone was clapping around me—the lecture had ended.

"That was so fascinating," Mackenzie said.

"I know," Sam said.

Colin kept clapping. "I'm really glad we came."

A crowd gathered around Leo, near the podium, and Josh stood beside him.

Mackenzie elbowed me. "Check out his grandson."

"I did," I agreed with a smile.

Sam gave me a harsh look. I shrugged. "He's cute," I said, the phrase *kissing cousins* flitting through my mind.

"We should go meet them," Sam said casually, and the four of us made our way toward the throng of people surrounding Leo.

Students asked Leo his position on various things—expressionism, cubism, painters I'd never heard of.

"But according to the Fauvists . . . " a student in a plaid shirt quizzed Leo.

"No, no, I disagree—" another student said. "Think of post-impressionist . . . "

I tried to think of ways to pipe in with, "But how do you feel about chocolate?"

Josh had drifted apart from the crowd—I wasn't sure if I was imagining it, but I thought he was staring at my sister. I moved closer to him and said, "Your grandfather gave a great lecture."

"I'm glad you liked it. Do you—are you a student here?"

"No . . . I'm, uh . . . " I waved Sam, Mackenzie, and Colin over. "I'm Sophie, and this is my sister Sam, and our friends Colin and Mackenzie. My sister and I just moved to Venice a couple of months ago."

I wasn't imagining it—he was definitely eyeing my sister. His cheeks flushed. He dug his hands deep into his pockets and beamed at her.

"We moved here from Cleveland," I said. "Does your, uh . . . does the rest of your family live in Indiana?"

"My parents live in Chicago, and Leo lives in Bloomington."

His parents! Even more Shattenbergs!

"Does your grandfather live by himself?" I asked.

Josh nodded. "My grandmother passed away a long time ago, before I was born."

"Oh, I'm sorry to hear that," I said.

"And are you in school in Venice?" he asked Sam, with a shy grin.

"I just finished college . . . I work for a private detective now," she said.

"Oh, wow," Josh said. "You must have lots of stories to tell—chasing after criminals? Catching murderers? Solving mysteries?" He rocked back on his feet, awaiting

55

thrilling stories from my sister.

"Our agency specializes in missing persons. Last month we located a girl who'd been missing from town for weeks—she'd been kidnapped," she told him.

Josh's eyes widened as she ran through the story of the Noelle case, and how we'd come to work for Gus Jenkins.

"These two are the Sherlock Holmeses of the Midwest," Colin said, putting his hand on my shoulder.

"We deduced that the fiend had been in our midst," I said in the best Sherlock Holmes voice I could muster.

Josh laughed. "You know—I'd like to introduce you to my grandfather." He led us over to Leo. A student was asking Leo about Israeli artists.

"Uh—sorry to interrupt, but I wanted to introduce you to these people from Venice," Josh told him. "Sophie, Mackenzie, Colin—and Sam." His voice lingered on Sam's name.

"Pleased to meet you," Leo said. He shook my hand with his soft palm. So many questions and comments flooded my brain that I stood with my mouth open, unable to speak.

He let go of my hand and shook Mackenzie's. "Your talk was so great," she said.

"It was . . . it's true what you said about art transcending cultures and time," Colin said.

"I know!" I said, catching my breath. "The other day I was reading about chocolate . . . "

They looked at me.

"How chocolate . . . has transcended . . . cultures and time."

Everyone stared at me as if I was crazy.

Sam jumped in. "I think my sister is talking about how that artist Janine Antoni used chocolate as her medium . . . isn't that what you meant?"

I nodded. "Right. Exactly."

Colin said, "I read about that artist—she chewed chocolate and exhibited it, didn't she?"

"She did," Sam said.

Leo shook Sam's hand then, and Josh said, "Sam works for a detective agency which specializes in missing persons." Josh's eyebrows floated upward.

Leo cocked his head and nodded slowly.

"My grandfather has a missing persons case," Josh explained.

"Josh—I don't know if . . . " Leo trailed off.

"Maybe they can help," Josh said. "One of the paintings my grandfather mentioned in his talk is in the Aldredge Art Museum in Indianapolis right now. My grandfather knows this painting belongs to someone else. We think it was stolen," Josh said.

"Stolen?" I breathed. "From who?"

"It belonged to the family of a woman named Ruth Brauner. We were childhood sweethearts." Leo smiled faintly. "Her family was friends with Sebrid and he gave the painting to them. Her family never would've parted with it willingly. Ruth told me her family had found a safe place for it during the war. She was certain it would be secure."

"How did it end up in the museum, then? Did her family sell it after the war?" Colin asked.

Leo shook his head. "I'm not sure how it made its way to this museum. Unfortunately Ruth's family was killed. Only she survived. I'm afraid the painting was misappropriated during the war somehow." He glanced at the empty chairs in the room. "I'd like to find Ruth. When the painting resurfaced . . . I took it as a sign that I should start searching for her again."

"You've looked for her yourselves, then?" Sam asked.

Josh nodded. "We've tried the Internet and public records, but we can't track her down. We even asked around for her at several homes for the elderly in Chicago—Chicago was where Leo last saw her. But we can't find her. She might be living under a different name. Or . . . she might have died even. But we'd like to find out. If that's the case, then her heirs, if she has any, may be entitled to the painting."

"I've read about a case like that," Colin said. "The Seattle Art Museum returned a painting a few years ago which the Nazis had stolen from a Jewish art dealer, right?"

"Yes." Leo smiled. "That's right. It was *Odalisque* by Matisse."

"Was that kind of theft really common?" Mackenzie asked.

Leo nodded. "Before and during the war, the Nazis seized a half-million important works of art. Afterward the Allies reclaimed a lot of it, but thousands of works were lost—either they were never recovered, never returned to their rightful owners, or destroyed. Many paintings found their way into legitimate art markets, including dealers, collectors, and museums."

"We think that might have happened to Ruth's painting," Josh said.

"Did Ruth have proof it belonged to her family?" Sam asked.

"The painting was signed and dedicated to the Brauner family on the back of the canvas," Leo said. "I talked to the curator at the museum, but he was brusque. He said there was no such signature. He said the painting legitimately belonged to the current owner, who loaned it to the museum for the show. But he wouldn't tell me who the current owner was."

"The painting's worth over a million dollars," Josh said.

The crowd had thinned out by now, and we sat down in the folding chairs facing one another. I stared at the colorful Israeli folk art on the walls.

Josh told Leo how we'd found Noelle, after the police had failed to.

"I've thought of hiring a detective," Leo said. "But I'm not sure if it would help. I don't even know if she's still alive. It's been over fifty years since I last saw Ruth." He said her name so softly now that you could barely hear it, and afterward looked down at his feet.

"How did you meet Ruth?" I asked.

"We were in school together in Vienna—we quickly became sweethearts. After the war we found each other again at a displaced persons camp in Stockholm. We decided to come to America, to start our new lives here. I found work in Chicago, and we moved there. We had plans to get married, after I saved a little money. Then one day she disappeared." He threw up his hands.

"Why?" Sam asked.

He shook his head. "The night before she went missing, I went to her boardinghouse after work. She was upset, talking in circles, not making any sense. I asked her to slow down, to tell me what had happened, and she mumbled something about *Lovers in the Village*. That was the title of the Sebrid painting her family owned."

Leo had shown a slide of that painting—candles burned in one corner, a fiddler played on a mountain in another, and in the middle of the painting a man and woman kissed above the rooftops of a village.

"She wouldn't tell me anything else. The next day, she disappeared. I tried to find her. I talked to her friends, her employer, her favorite shopkeepers, but they were just as surprised and confused as I was. I made up posters and put them around town. I took out an ad in the *Chicago Sentinel*. I filed a missing persons report with the police. I went to the courthouse, looking for any public records of Ruth, hoping they'd lead me to something—and this was the strange thing. They had no record of a Ruth Brauner even existing. It was all so incomprehensible. A complete mystery." Leo rested his hands in his lap. His fingers were long and thin, like my father's.

He stared down at his black shoes. "It took me a long time to recover from that loss. After everything—we'd been so grateful to have each other, to be starting our new lives together in this new country, this unknown place. When she disappeared with no explanation—well. I was never quite the same after that."

Hearing him talk about Ruth like this made me think about the friends I'd left behind in New York. The fact that Leo missed Ruth so much, and still clearly loved her, was somehow comforting. If he'd never forgotten her after she'd disappeared, then maybe Viv would never forget me either. And if Leo could still be reunited with Ruth . . . maybe I'd see Viv again someday, too.

"I think we can help you," Sam said. Her face was rosy and alive, her eyes dancing at the prospect of this case. "We can meet and discuss it with Gus Jenkins, the head of our agency. At the very least, we might be able to find out the ownership history of the painting."

"That sounds like a great idea, doesn't it?" Josh asked Leo.

"It does," Leo said. He looked hopeful. I was ecstatically grateful to Sam—if we took on this case, we could find out even more about Leo and Josh. It was the perfect excuse for getting further information without blowing our cover.

Sam gave Leo and Josh her business card—it matched the stationery she'd had printed up—and took down their phone numbers as well.

"It was so great to meet you," I said to Leo and Josh as we got ready to leave.

"Thank you for a great lecture," Mackenzie said.

"You're welcome," Leo said. "Thank you."

I wanted to say something else, to hug them, or something, but I wasn't sure what.

"We'll be in touch," Sam told them, and we shook hands good-bye.

4

"Now we just have to convince Gus to take on the case," Sam said as we walked back to the car.

Glowing streetlamps dotted the campus; we passed a dorm window blaring the Grateful Dead. "He'll take it on," I said. "He doesn't have any other cases right now. All he's got is a pile of notes in Russian."

"Don't remind me," Sam said.

I could hardly wait for Mackenzie to drop us off so Sam and I could talk about our new relatives. When we finally said good night and trotted up our front porch, I told Sam, "Our cousin is in love with you."

She kicked off her shoes. "What?"

"The boy looked totally smitten with you," I said.

She glanced at me sideways. "No, he didn't."

"He kept staring at you the whole time!"

"You're crazy." She flipped through the mail.

"It's too bad he's our cousin," I said.

"Yeah. May be our cousin."

"It's a shame we didn't relocate to Arkansas instead of Indiana," I said. "I've heard this kind of thing is pretty

62

common there."

"You're sick. And hillbilly-ist," she said.

"Hillbilly-ist?"

"Yeah. Holier-than-thou toward hillbillies."

"Okay. You can join the Wilshire College Coalition Against Hillbilly-ist-ism, then. The WCCAH. I think I saw a flyer for it," I said.

"Can't wait to sign up." She leafed through a Morningstar mutual funds newsletter.

"You and Josh would have really cute three-eyed children."

She squinted at me. "I'm glad you're enjoying this."

We met Gus for brunch at the Petal Diner the following morning. He stumbled in at a quarter to eleven, unshaven and with a coffee stain the size of Texas on his light blue shirt.

"I hope this is important," he grumbled as he slid into the booth. "Getting me up at this hour on a Saturday morning."

"This hour? It's eleven o'clock," Sam said.

"My car's out of gas . . . spilled coffee down my shirt walking here . . . " Gus began to grouch unintelligibly. "I need coffee, Wilda!"

Wilda glanced at us from another table. She wore her usual green eye shadow, and a necklace strung with red beads and little ceramic black cats. The cats resembled her own cat, Betty, who blinked at us from a stool by the counter.

"Wilda!" Gus yelled.

"All right, all right." Wilda ambled over in her pink

apron. "Someone's a bundle of sweetness and charm this morning." She glared at him.

"I also need some blueberry pancakes, tall stack, pronto," he ordered.

"Watch your manners," Wilda said, pulling the coffeepot away from his mug.

"Please," he mumbled.

Wilda filled his cup. "That's better."

Sam ordered blueberry pancakes as well, and I ordered chocolate chip ones. After gulping his coffee down in three seconds, Gus excused himself to the bathroom.

"How's it going, working for Gus?" Wilda asked us as she refilled his mug. "Find any dinosaur bones buried under that mess in his office?"

"I found a pair of 'Merry Christmas' boxer shorts filed under '1999 Tax Return,'" Sam said.

"Oh yuck," I said at the thought of Gus's underwear.

"Must have gotten a great tax refund that year," Wilda said.

Gus returned from the bathroom and settled back into the booth. After Wilda brought over our breakfasts, Sam rearranged her silverware.

"We've got a new case for you," she told Gus.

"Don't tell me. Some cheerleader in town has gotten abducted and the only evidence is a pair of pom-poms," Gus said. He poured a long stream of white sugar into his coffee.

"This is serious," Sam said. "We met a man at a lecture last night at Wilshire College who has a missing persons case." She filled Gus in on everything Leo had told us about Ruth and the painting.

Gus rubbed his forehead.

"So what do you think?" I asked him.

He shrugged. "I don't know."

"What don't you know?" I asked. "This case has everything—romance, intrigue, stolen art, and the war."

Gus took a huge bite of pancakes. "We're not producing a movie here. We're detectives," he barked at me, his mouth full.

"I know that. I think it's a worthwhile and important case," I said.

Sam rested her elbows on the table. "What are your reservations?"

Gus waved his fork. "These kinds of cases are complicated. First off, you say he hasn't been in touch with this Ruth broad for fifty years. It's not easy to track someone down after so long—she most likely has a different last name now—or she could be dead."

"Or she could be alive," I said.

"There's a small chance of that," he admitted. "But finding a broad—"

"I wish you'd stop saying 'broad,'" I said. "It makes us sound like we're in a B-movie."

Gus rolled his eyes. "Finding a lovely lady like Ruth who's been missing for fifty years . . . he doesn't need a detective, he needs a magician."

"I think it's worth a try," Sam said. "At the very least we can check into the background of the painting."

Sam and I'd decided that we should focus on the painting aspect of the case with Gus, since the prospect of recovering a million-dollar painting was more likely to entice him than the idea of reuniting long-lost loves.

"Say we look into the painting's ownership history and we don't find anything pointing to this broad. Lady. Did you secure a retainer from Shutterbug?" he asked.

"Shattenberg," I said.

"You need to go over specifics before you agree to do any work," Gus went on. "No retainer, and no results, then some clients don't pay. I only work for pay."

"We didn't talk about money," Sam said in a low voice. "But I think he'll pay for it. I don't think he was under the impression that our services are free."

"Did you discuss our standard contract?" Gus asked.

"Standard contract? The other day I found a 1983 issue of *Playboy* in the file where your standard contracts are supposed to be." She threw her crumpled napkin at him.

Gus lowered his eyes and perused the dessert menu. "That wasn't mine." He coughed. "Well, we need to draw up a contract, then. Get the business end of things in order." He downed his second cup of coffee in one long chug. "If we take on the case."

"It's not as if we have a hundred other clients lining up at our door." Sam fiddled with the salt and pepper shakers, making them touch side by side. "I think we should vote on it. All employees of Gus Jenkins and Associates who vote in favor of taking on the Leo Shattenberg case say 'Aye.'"

"Aye!" I said.

"Aye!" Sam said.

Gus shook his head. "Lord help me," he moaned as Wilda came over to our table.

"More coffee?" she asked us.

"Please," Gus said. "And a piece of that blackberry pie, too. I need something to console myself with. I just lost control of my own agency."

As we left the diner, Sam paused to button her jacket—the heat wave had broken—and I stared at the calendar Wilda had hung up by the cash register. It featured cats dressed in different outfits; September was a Siamese in a wedding veil. Below the picture something caught my eye—Rosh Hashanah, the Jewish New Year, a couple weeks away.

Visiting the Hillel and all these thoughts of the Shattenbergs being our relatives had made me feel this strange longing to be, well, more Jewish. I wished that we could celebrate Rosh Hashanah. Our family wasn't that religious, but on Rosh Hashanah we always had a traditional meal with apples dipped in honey so the new year would be sweet. My shoulders slumped as I thought how we wouldn't be able to celebrate it now, at least not in any open way. Here we were on the brink of confirming that we did have some relatives in the world—but could we ever act like we were family?

Sam interrupted my thoughts. "So how do you feel about taking a trip to the Aldredge Museum this afternoon?"

We called Colin and Mackenzie to see if they wanted to join us, and before we knew it the four of us were on our way to Indianapolis. The Aldredge Art Museum was just outside of the city, in a large white mansion with huge columns in front. A garden with perfectly manicured hedges and flower beds lined the pathway to the main door. Mackenzie had been to the museum before, with her mom.

"It used to belong to a millionaire named Isabella Aldredge," she said. "She designated the mansion to become a museum after she died."

At the information desk we asked, "Could you tell us where we could find the Ivan Sebrid painting?"

The lady at the desk gave us a pamphlet with a floor plan to the museum, and pointed us toward the Harleman Gallery. We walked through another gallery on the way that was dedicated to Bruce Busby, the famous sculptor. "My mom loves his work," Mackenzie said. The gallery featured a range of Busby's sculptures and drawings, including one large tentlike sculpture, thirty feet high and peaked at the top like a New Age cathedral. The outside was covered with geometrical designs in various colors.

We reached *Lovers in the Village* and stood before it. It was smaller than I'd thought it would be, in an ornate gold frame. The colors were so much brighter in person, and the kiss more prominent—the couple's eyes were exaggerated and their lips barely touched.

When I'd visited my mom at her art gallery, she'd always said that to really see a painting you had to stand back and not just look at the center, but to peel your eyes away and really absorb the whole thing. I stepped back and took in the fiddler and the candles and the village—under the eaves of one roof I noticed a tiny Star of David.

I wondered what it would mean to Ruth to have this

painting back, something that had probably symbolized so much to her and her family. I thought of all the things we'd left behind in our house in Queens—paintings, furniture, tchotchkes, books, my dad's sweaters that I'd borrowed on winter mornings.

"We need to get that guard out of the room," Sam whispered.

"You think we should take a look at the back of the painting?" Colin asked.

Sam nodded.

The guard kept eyeing us. He was young, not much older than I was, and short—even shorter than me, and I was only five-two. He had a tuft of scraggly black hair on his chin—you could tell he probably thought that was really attractive—and a mouth full of brownish teeth.

The four of us wandered through the next two adjoining rooms and into the hallway, to talk.

"What should we do?" I asked them. "How can we check the back of the painting with the guard standing right there?"

"We have to distract him," Sam said. She stared at me.

"No," I told her.

"No what?"

"You're looking at me in that way. I know you've got some crazy idea that I've got to do. You probably want me to go on a date with him or something." A month ago it had been Sam's idea for me to go on that date with Troy Howard, to gather information about Noelle. Of course, I'd been longing to go out with him anyway,

69

so it had been convenient. But I was certainly not long-ing to go out with a brown-toothed security guard.

"I was just thinking you should talk to this guard a little, use your feminine wiles and whatnot. Just . . . say something that would make him leave the room so we could take a look at the back."

I folded my arms. "No way. He looks like a garden gnome. And why do I have to be the one to do this?"

Colin looked especially amused. "He's not your type?"

"No."

"My mom told me a lot of the guards here are aspir-ing artists," Mackenzie said. "We can tell him we're art students and we've got a question about the owner of the painting. We'll tell him we're doing a research proj-ect on Sebrid and we need his help. We'll flirt and get him to cough up some information."

Some of the guys I knew at LaGuardia had worked as guards in the Metropolitan Museum. "I guess we could try it, if you're willing to do it with me."

"I don't mind," Mackenzie told me. "It's for a good cause."

I smoothed my hair, we took deep breaths, and approached the Gnome.

His dark eyes followed our every move in the room.

"Hi," Mackenzie said. "We're doing a project for school on that painting over there, by Ivan Sebrid? We were wondering if you could help us . . . if you could tell us who the owner is?"

I tried to remember everything I'd learned from a *Cosmo* article I'd read on line at the supermarket,

"A Hundred Tips on Flirting." Make eye contact. Smile often. Ask questions. Unfortunately they hadn't given any specific advice for flirting with men resembling garden ornaments.

"Nope. That's private information," he said. The tuft on his chin bobbed as he spoke.

"But we have this school project," I said. "It's really important." I made eye contact and smiled. "Are you an art student?"

"How'd ya know?" He grinned, exposing his brown teeth.

"You look . . . artistic," I said. "What medium do you work in?"

"I'm a sculptor." The tuft bobbed. "I make caves out of old magazines—you can actually walk in them and stuff. I use old magazines like *Penthouse* and *Monster Trucks* and stack them up and shellac them."

"Wow, that sounds amazing." I tried to sound sincerely enthused.

"Maybe we could see your work sometime," Mackenzie gushed.

"Ya wanna?"

"We'd love to," I said, forcing a smile. "But do you think you could help us with our research?"

He leaned closer. "What do ya need?" His breath was not exactly fragrant.

"Could you find out the name of the owner for us? We promise we won't tell a soul. Our teacher told us we're supposed to write a little bit about the provenance of the painting." I said *provenance* with a French accent, in a lame attempt to sound sophisticated.

71

The Gnome grinned. He seemed impressed. "Well. I guess I could maybe do that. They keep a file on that in the office."

I leaned toward him. "I promise we'll make it worth your while." I'd heard that line used on *General Hospital*.

His grin grew wider and wider, as if he'd just won the lottery. "Okay. I'll go and see what I can find out. I get off work in two hours. You girls wanna meet me out front then, and we can go to my studio?"

"That's a fabulous idea," Mackenzie said.

He walked down the hall, and we waved Sam and Colin in from the next room. We all scampered to the painting.

Colin was about to touch the frame when Sam whispered, "Wait! Stop! We need to check if there's an alarm." She waved her hands around the painting in spastic motions, and then quickly jabbed the frame. I held my breath. Nothing happened.

"I guess they have the alarm turned off during the day. Okay. Let's do it." She lifted one end and Colin lifted the other—it took a minute to maneuver it off the wall. We looked at the back.

Completely blank. The back of the canvas was old and weathered, dirty and brown, but there was no signature—nothing.

"Oh no," I said.

Sam shook her head. "This sucks."

They put it back on the wall just as footsteps clomped down the hall. Sam and Colin scurried out.

"I found out one thing for ya," the Gnome said. "The

owner's name is Dale DeCarlo. He owns a lot of stuff we show here, and at the Indy Museum of Art, too. I hope this helps with your project."

"It's great," I said. "Thanks so much."

"My name's Orin, by the way. I didn't catch yours."

"I'm . . . Nancy," I said. "And this is Bess."

"Nancy and Bess. Great to meet y'all. So ya gonna meet me out front in two hours?"

"Can't wait," Mackenzie said.

"Looking forward to it," I said. My stomach turned at the thought. We'd be happily settled back in Venice by then. "See you!" I said.

We marched out of the gallery and met my sister and Colin in the hall.

"So why isn't there any signature?" Sam asked.

I shrugged. "The canvas looked old, like it was the original."

We walked down the marble corridors. I stopped at the gift shop and bought a postcard of the Sebrid painting, and then we headed out toward the car.

"At least we got a hot date out of the whole deal," Mackenzie said. I moaned and shivered at the thought. We gave Sam and Colin the recap of our whole conversation with the Gnome.

"Poor Orin, he's going to wait outside in two hours and not know what happened," Colin said.

I opened the car door. "He'll survive. He can return to his magazine cave."

We'd just stepped in the door to our house when the phone rang. Sam picked it up.

"Oh, hi, Josh," she said, her eyes widening. I ran upstairs to get on the extension.

"I've got good news—we talked to Gus and he wants to take on the case," she told him. She left out the description of us outvoting him so that we at least appeared to be professional.

"So when do you want to get together?" Josh asked.

"Well, let's see." I heard pages fluttering. "Are you free Wednesday evening?" she asked. "We could meet you at Wilshire again, or here in Venice."

"Oh, we can't Wednesday. My grandfather has band practice. He plays clarinet in a klezmer band."

"Oh, I love klezmer," Sam said.

"You know klezmer?"

I stared at the phone. I almost never heard Sam slip. Klezmer was this raucous Yiddish music, and if we weren't Jewish we probably wouldn't know about it. Sam and I'd heard the band the Klezmatics play outside the Jewish Museum at New York City's Museum Mile festival in May.

"Oh—I heard a band play that kind of music in Cleveland once." She quickly changed the subject. "So okay, Wednesday's out. How about later in the week?"

"My grandfather's giving a talk at a conference at Kenyon College in Ohio, so he'll be gone late that week and over the weekend. Then I've got a huge philosophy exam the twenty-fifth, and study groups every night. I guess my grandfather could meet you without me, but he said he'd like for me to be there."

"And you want to be there because you like my sister," I wanted to say.

"How about the next weekend, then?" Sam asked.

"Um, that's a holiday—Rosh Hashanah—the Jewish New Year. We're having a dinner here . . . maybe you and your sister and your boss could come to the dinner, and we can talk about the case afterward?"

"That's really nice of you to invite us, but we can just meet another time . . . " Sam was probably making a list in her head of all the reasons why we shouldn't go: it would be hard to keep our cover and pretend we didn't know what was going on; Gus would likely object, saying it was unnecessary and unprofessional. . . .

Before I could stop myself I said: "We'd love to go!"

"Who's that?" Josh asked.

"It's me—Sophie—I'm on the extension."

"Oh, hi, Sophie," Josh said. "I didn't know you were there."

"I think we should go—it sounds like fun," I said.

"Great," Josh said. "We'll see you here at seven?"

"Okay," Sam said hesitantly. I was clearly going to be in for it when we got off the phone. "Should we bring anything?"

"No—we'll have everything prepared. Have you ever been to a Rosh Hashanah dinner?"

"No, never," Sam lied.

"I hope you like it. We'll see you then."

We said good-bye. Sam met me at the bottom of the stairs, with a hand on her hip. "Sophie. I can't believe you just did that."

"What?" I shrugged. "So we go to the dinner and spend more time with them, learn more about them. It was the polite thing to do, to accept his invitation."

75

"Polite?" She squinted at me. "You just want to eat apples and honey and challah bread, and ask more surreptitious are-you-my-relative questions."

"Basically, yeah."

She sighed. "I can't imagine Gus at a Rosh Hashanah dinner."

I smiled, thinking about it. "Brooke ata adenoid gland . . . " I imitated him reading a Hebrew prayer.

"You're going to have to say the prayer like that, too, Fiona Scott," she told me.

"No problem. And I can't wait to try that 'cholla' bread." I pronounced the *ch* in the normal English way, like in *chair*.

"Cholla. Sounds delicious," Sam said.

5

"I still don't see the point of going to this Husharana whatever. We're a detective agency. We don't make house calls. Especially on other people's holidays." Gus had been grumbling during the whole drive to Wilshire College for the Rosh Hashanah dinner.

"Stop complaining," Sam told him. "I know you have more experience than we do, but the fact is your case list for the past year has been . . . a little slow, to put it nicely. So I think accepting our clients' invitation, and spending a little time with them before they sign the contract, is a good idea."

Gus chewed a stick of nicotine gum. He wore a plaid suit jacket for the occasion that looked like it was from 1965. "Speaking of signing the contract, let me state again that doing the detective work before the contract is signed is not how we work at the Jenkins Agency."

Sam rolled her eyes. Gus had been sore that we'd checked out the painting without him.

"I bet there'll be some really good food tonight," I said, thinking the mention of a feast would put Gus in a better mood. "And lots of wine, too."

His ears perked a little. "Better be good food. I'm famished."

Josh greeted us at the door. *"L'shanah tovah!"* He shook our hands. "That means 'Happy New Year.'"

I knew what it meant, but I nodded as if I didn't. "Happy New Year," Sam and I told him.

Leo shook our hands. A part of me wanted to hug Leo and Josh, I was so excited to see them. We introduced them to Gus.

"Uh, happy holiday," Gus told them awkwardly.

Tables were set up inside; Josh had saved seats for the three of us. I was seated next to Gus, across from Leo. Josh sat between Leo and Sam.

Gus eyed a loaf of bread under a prayer cloth and reached for it.

"No!" I said before I could stop myself—you weren't supposed to eat the bread until the prayer was said, but of course I wasn't supposed to know that. I tried to save face. "You shouldn't fill up on bread before dinner, Gus, really."

He looked at me like I was insane.

"Actually," Josh said, "we need to say the *motzi* first, the blessing of the bread, before we eat it."

"Oh, sorry," Gus said grumpily.

The dinner began with the lighting of the candles, and the prayer.

Baruch atah Adonai, elohaynu, melech ha-olam . . .

Gus scratched his ear in silence. We poured wine— sweet Manischewitz, which I loved—and Josh said the evening kiddush, the prayer over the wine, and then the *motzi,* and the blessing for apples and honey, for a sweet new year.

"Also on the table are pomegranates, the symbol of plenty, and carrots, which symbolize the Yiddish word *merren* which means 'more'," Josh explained. "We want more of all the good things in life. For Sephardic Jews, carrots are symbolic of the phrase *Yikaretu oyveychem,* which means 'may your enemies be cut down.' We ask that those who wish bad for us not get their wish, that they don't succeed."

"Yickyray oy vay," I deliberately mispronounced, thinking of Enid.

"Pretty different from midnight drinking and football, all this," Gus said, pouring himself another glass of Manischewitz.

I eavesdropped on Josh and Sam as we ate. "So how do you like your first Rosh Hashanah?" Josh asked her.

"It's great," Sam said.

"Tomorrow afternoon is *Tashlikh,*" he said. "It means 'casting off.' You're supposed to walk to a creek, or any body of water, and throw bread crumbs in, to symbolize casting off all your mistakes of last year, and starting over."

"Really," Sam said, sounding intrigued. She looked sincerely ignorant.

"There's this really pretty creek on campus . . . " Josh said.

It was time to get some more information from Leo. I smoothed the skirt I'd worn for the occasion, a long, demure-looking flower print I'd bought at Second Hand Rose, a thrift shop in downtown Venice. I thought it was a good I-might-be-your-relative skirt. "I've seen lots of butterflies around here . . . they're so pretty, aren't they? Do you like butterflies?"

Leo paused. "Yes . . . butterflies are very pretty."

"I mean . . . do you really like butterflies? Do you collect them?"

"I like them, but no, I don't collect them."

My stomach sank. I was sure my dad had said that our Leo had collected butterflies.

Then he added, "I did as a little boy, though."

"Sam," I said, interrupting her conversation with Josh. "Leo collected butterflies."

"Really?" Sam said.

"Very long ago," Leo said.

Gus gave me a strange look, as if to say, "Why on earth do you care if this man collected butterflies?"

"I love the apples and honey," I said. "But it would be so great if we had chocolate with this, too. Don't you think?"

"Chocolate would be nice," Leo said. "But apples and honey are the traditional foods."

"Oh, of course," I said. "But chocolate would still be really good. Wilda, at the Petal Diner? She makes this amazing chocolate cake—you'll have to come try it sometime."

"I would like that," Leo said.

"Also, you know, you remember our friend Colin, who came to your lecture? He runs a bike shop. Do you like to bicycle?"

"Not at my age," Leo said, and laughed. The bottle of wine on the table had run out, and Leo excused himself to the kitchen to get another.

Gus squinted at me. "Butterflies? Chocolate? Bi-cycling? Why are you peppering this poor guy with these crazy questions? Look, he had to run off to get away from you." He stared at my glass. "How much did you have to drink?"

"Nothing—like two sips. This is detective work," I told him assuredly. "I'm trying to find out things about his personality."

Gus shook his head. "You got a lot to learn about detecting, my dear."

I realized I sounded ridiculous—but I knew he had to be our relative. I just knew it. I longed to admit to Leo that we were Jewish, that we understood everything going on . . . to be accepted as part of the traditions instead of viewed as outsiders. But at least we were celebrating Rosh Hashanah—it was better than doing nothing, or just baking a loaf of honeycake and scarfing it down by ourselves at home.

Leo came back to the table with another bottle. Josh and my sister were talking quietly together.

"So you'd like us to find your old sweetheart," Gus said, getting down to business. He gave me a look as if to say, "Watch a pro."

At least he used the word *sweetheart* instead of *broad*.

"The girls told me about Brauner mentioning the painting before she disappeared," Gus said.

Sam and I told Leo and Josh how we'd seen the paint-ing in the museum and looked at the back, but hadn't found a signature.

"It's possible the painting was relined or the signature

removed," Gus said. "Can you tell us any other details you remember about Brauner's disappearance?"

Leo leaned back in his chair. "Let's see. It wasn't long after we came to Chicago. The night after she was upset about the painting—it was a Friday, I remember because I came home early from my job for the Shabbos dinner Ruth always cooked for us at her boardinghouse kitchen—and she was gone. Her suitcase, her favorite dress, the few things she owned—all had disappeared. Another boarder, a girl, Frankie Weinstein, she told me Ruth had left that day. Frankie had seen Ruth with another man."

"Really," I said. It was like a tragic soap opera.

His voice was low; he held his palms up helplessly as he talked. "I wanted to speak to Ruth. I didn't believe this other-man story—what other man? Ruth didn't know any other men. We loved each other." His voice grew soft, and he stared down at the table. "I tried to find her. Ruth had given a phone number to Frankie, but it was the wrong number. I looked everywhere, drove around the streets, tried all her friends. Some of her friends helped me search, too, but we found nothing. Ruth had disappeared without a trace." He reached into his pocket. "I brought this, to show you."

He pulled out a black-and-white photo of a young couple: a man with a full head of dark hair and a pretty young woman in his arms.

"That was Ruth and me." He passed the photo around to us. I held it like a robin's egg. The edges were crumbling and the backing was peeling off; this was a photo that had been pored over and loved. In the picture Leo and Ruth clasped each other tightly; Ruth's head rested against Leo's chest.

"I know it sounds like a cliché, but I never stopped loving her. Everyone back then . . . I can't describe what it was like after the war. But Ruth and I had happy times. She worked at Wieboldt's Department Store and every day I'd pick her up after work and we'd go have ice creams at Barish's drugstore. After she disappeared I kept going to Barish's every afternoon, hoping I'd see her, for two years. I never saw her again."

His cheeks sagged as he put the photo back in his chest pocket.

"Eventually, I tried to get used to life without her. I met Judy Bowolski, and we were happy—we had a wonderful son and grandson." He touched Josh's shoulder. "Judy died almost thirty years ago. Now, after seeing the painting—I keep thinking about Ruth again. I simply have a feeling that she still might be alive."

"We'll find her," I said. "I know we will." I didn't care if Gus considered finding her a remote possibility. We'd do it somehow. My confidence was bolstered by the fact that Leo had the same blind faith in Ruth's existence that I had toward the possibility of him being our relative.

We finished the main course and salad, and moved on to dessert. I was so full I thought I was going to burst the seam of my skirt. Josh brought out coffee.

"Mr. Shattenberg? Should we move to another room to discuss a few specifics?" Gus asked Leo. Then he nodded toward Sam, who pulled out the contract and handed it to him. Gus and Leo took their coffee mugs to the library to sign the papers.

Josh went back to the kitchen and returned with a handful of Hershey's Kisses, which he gave to me. "You asked about chocolate, so I thought you might want some. My grandfather loves these. Do you know he told me he used to take the rationed chocolate bars he received from the Red Cross and whittle them into little shapes to give Ruth."

I gave Sam a look. *Chocolate. See?*

Josh put a Hershey's Kiss in Sam's palm and let his fingers linger there for a second.

I raised my eyebrows at her. She pretended not to notice and walked over to the library, where Leo was writing Gus a check. Leo and Gus shook hands, and Gus stood up to leave.

Josh said to Sam, "So I'll see you at the *Tashlikh* tomorrow, at four?"

"Okay," Sam said. Maybe it was the wine, or the dinner, or my growing conviction that Leo and Josh were our relatives—but when we said good night I gave them both huge hugs good-bye.

As we walked back to the car Gus said, "All right, girls, Lesson One in detective work. Fraternizing with the clients is not a good idea."

"What are you talking about?" Sam asked.

"First off, you," he said to me, "with the chocolate and butterflies and whatever cock-and-bull questions you were drilling this man with, and telling him you're sure we'll find her. No more wine for you ever. And you," he said to Sam, "going to do the Tashkent with the grandson! Don't think I didn't hear that."

84

This was more paternal than Gus had ever seemed before.

"We're just finding out more information," Sam said. "We're getting to know the clients."

"I don't know if we should trust this grandson of his. College boys—you can't trust college boys."

"I'm twenty-one years old! I think I can make decisions by myself. And anyway, it's not romantic or anything. I'm just finding out more about them, for the case."

"For the case," Gus said skeptically.

"For the case," Sam repeated.

Gus climbed into the front seat. "And I'm afraid to tell you what I think happened the day this Brauner broad disappeared."

"What?" I asked him, my stomach quivering. Had Gus already figured everything out?

"I think she got the painting back that day, cashed it in, left our fine client, and skipped town with her new beau. That's what I think."

"You're so unromantic," I said. "Haven't you ever heard of true love?"

"Not in this lifetime," Gus grumped.

Wilda had told us that Gus's wife left him years ago. Obviously the experience hadn't exactly turned him into a starry-eyed dreamer.

I called Mackenzie when we got home and told her about the dinner, and Gus's theory about the painting and Ruth's disappearance.

"I talked to my mom about the whole thing, too," she

said. "She's heard of Dale DeCarlo, and he's supposed to be pretty shady. His father, Roderick DeCarlo, was known to have criminal connections, and my mom said she wouldn't be surprised at all if that painting is stolen Holocaust art. Roderick DeCarlo was accused of dealing in stolen artwork a few times."

"I guess we better be careful when we go talk to him," I said.

"My mom told me she doesn't want me getting within a mile of that guy. But she does know someone we can talk to—she's friends with this art conservator, a woman named Susan MacDonald. They went to art school together. My mom says Susan might know how we could tell if the signature was removed from the back of the painting, or had faded or something. She gave me Susan's number so we can meet with her if we want."

"That would be great," I told her. "Maybe this weekend or something." I was beginning to think the Jenkins Agency should hire Mackenzie, too.

When I hung up the phone, I told Sam what Mackenzie had said.

"If DeCarlo has criminal connections, maybe our own criminal connection knows something about him," she said.

"Difriggio?"

She nodded. "We should pay him a visit this week and find out what he knows." She sank down in the couch. "And I've been thinking . . . you should come with me for the walk with Josh tomorrow."

"Why? Don't you want to be alone with him?"

"Well . . . not really. I mean, if you're there, then we

can both ask about their family history, and you can help me remember all the things he says."

"And you want me to keep you from making out with your cousin."

She gave me a hard stare.

We met up with Josh the next day, at the Wilshire Student Union. Students ambled around, carrying doughnuts and coffee cups. A whole row of tables was set up for Peace and Justice Week, with petitions to be signed and postcards to send to Congress. Josh stood in front of the information desk. He wore a dark green sweater and jeans.

"Hi!" Sam said to him, her voice wavering like a teenage boy hitting puberty.

Josh kissed her on the cheek, and she turned an inhuman shade of red. Her mouth opened, then closed again. She twirled her hair—Sam never twirled her hair. She was nervous. Terrified, to be exact.

I finally figured out what was going on: my sister liked our cousin. No wonder she wanted a chaperon. Not only did she need some reminding that he most likely shared several genes with us, but she was probably nervous from lack of experience with any guy who liked her. She'd never dated anyone before. Not that I was the Dating Queen myself, but I had absorbed copious amounts of information from years of reading *Cosmo* and *Seventeen*.

"Hi," Josh said to me quizzically.

"I, uh . . . I just thought Sophie would like to come, too," Sam said.

"Of course. Glad you're here," Josh said, but he didn't sound it.

It had drizzled all morning; Sam wore a forest green jacket and hiking boots. Even in New York City, Sam always dressed more like a park ranger than a city girl. She shoved her hands in the pockets of her jeans.

"You look pretty in green," he told her.

"Uh, thanks," she said awkwardly. "You look nice in green, too."

They both grinned like goofy toddlers. There was an awkward pause. They laughed, and stuffed their hands deeper in their pockets. This was embarrassing.

"Ready for our walk?" he asked.

We nodded. We strolled toward the woods behind the campus. "I like the idea of casting away your mistakes in the water," Sam said.

It was a nice idea, though we'd never done *Tashlikh* in Queens. The nearest body of water was the East River, and it was too far away, and polluted and pretty disgusting. What else could we do, toss crumbs in the sink?

We told Josh about our trip to the Aldredge Museum in more detail—how Mackenzie and I distracted the guard while Sam and Colin took the painting off the wall, and that we were going to try to meet with the art conservator on Sunday.

"Is Colin your boyfriend?" Josh asked Sam.

"No." She smiled. "He's just a friend."

"Do you have a boyfriend?" His voice was tentative.

"No," she said.

His shoulders relaxed; he must've been worried about that. I was already feeling like a major third wheel. I followed behind them as they talked about books—he'd read *Women and Economics* and also loved *Naked Economics* by Charles Wheelan. He was majoring in economics, actually.

"Do you ever watch *Wall $treet Week*?" she asked.

His eyes glinted. "I love that show."

I almost wanted to throw up. But I was enjoying the walk. The back campus of Wilshire College was beautiful—winding paths past trees and meadows and a horse pasture. I suddenly wanted to go to school there, it was so pretty. The creek ran through the woods, and flowering bushes dipped into it, dropping their petals onto the water. Josh picked a handful of raspberries and offered them to us, and I kept picking more as we walked. In a few minutes, we reached a spot where the creek widened and a patch of weeping willow trees grew.

"This is it," Josh said. "Now take a handful of crumbs and toss them into the water, along with all the memories from the past year you'd like to get rid of."

This past year: I didn't even know where to start. Our dad's death, Enid, taking the money and leaving home and starting over . . . I wondered if we'd ever be forgiven for what we did, and also if we could really cast off our old selves. Would we get caught? How bad was everything we'd done, really? Would we be punished for it, down the road? I felt like we'd already been punished enough.

I threw my crumbs in, thinking about the night our father died and the morning we left Queens. Sam threw hers in, too, and I imagined that she must have been remembering exactly the same things.

"So . . . Scott . . . is that Catholic? Protestant?" Josh asked.

"Oh . . . it's Protestant," Sam said, staring at the creek. "But our family wasn't religious at all."

"Did you have any Jewish friends growing up? I've heard there are lots of Jews in Cleveland."

"Yeah, we had some Jewish friends." Her voice sounded stiff, and hesitant. I could tell she wasn't sure what to say, and didn't want to give away too much.

"There aren't that many Jewish students at Wilshire. Enough for a Hillel, but still not too many. Some people are even outright anti-Semitic—my grandfather came and spoke on Holocaust Remembrance Day last spring. I was in a philosophy class at the time that was discussing the Holocaust, and this guy in the class said, 'I think Jews need to stop moaning about the Holocaust and just get on with it,' as if the Holocaust was something you could forget."

"That's completely ridiculous," Sam said sharply. "How could someone be so stupid and insensitive?"

I held my breath for a second, hoping that Josh wouldn't read too much into her reaction. He didn't say anything at first, he just stared at her with a mixture of surprise and appreciation.

"I know," he finally said, softly. "I thought the same thing. But you know, most people don't get it the way you do, unless they had family who died in it, too."

Sam looked back at Josh, and I knew how frustrated she must have felt at that moment, that she couldn't tell him why we understood.

I wanted to tell Josh that it was personal for us, too.

Even to say the word *Holocaust*—it meant something so different to Sam and me, and to Josh, than it did to most people. Those were our relatives who'd died, and even though I never knew them, as strange as it sounds, I still felt the loss of never having gotten to know them, of having so few relatives in the first place. It was like losing our parents was magnified so much, because we had no other relatives who could try to take their place. And that was because of the Holocaust, because we were Jewish, because so many of our relatives had been killed.

"Do you mind if I ask—who in your family died in the war?" Sam asked.

"My great-grandparents—Leo's aunts, and both his parents," Josh said. "And lots of cousins. But I'm actually not sure exactly who or how many. Leo doesn't really like to talk about it and I haven't been so great about keeping track of the lineage."

"Do you know their names?" Sam asked.

"I don't, actually. Why do you ask?"

"Oh, I don't know. Just curious."

"Are you related to any Heschels?" I asked.

Josh gave me a strange look. "I don't think there are any Heschels. You'd have to ask Leo."

I stared at the bottom of the creek. No Heschels? There had to be a Heschel in his family somewhere.

"I've read that there were a lot of people who were missing, too, whose deaths were never completely confirmed," Sam said. "Or some people who they thought died, but actually lived."

Josh led us away from the creek and down the path.

91

"That's true. So many people were killed that a lot of the places of death and dates of death are just a guess. My grandfather was never even sure what became of some of his relatives."

My heart quickened. "Do you know anything about Leo's extended family?"

Josh shook his head. "Not that much. He tried to track down some relatives after the war, but all were assumed to be dead. As I said, he doesn't like to talk about it much, either . . . I think it makes him too upset."

I wanted to quiz Josh on all his relatives' names, but I'd already pushed it enough. I couldn't have Josh figure out the real reason why I was asking.

As we walked down the path back toward the campus, the sky darkened and it began to drizzle again. We had two umbrellas between us, so Josh and Sam huddled under one and I lagged behind them. They talked and smiled and giggled—my sensible sister actually giggled.

When we reached the student center, we ordered cups of hot chocolate to go, and Sam said that it was time we headed back.

Josh gazed at her intensely, as if he could stare at her for hours. "I had a wonderful time," he said. "I hope . . . I hope I can see you again."

She nodded. "Thanks so much for inviting us. I'm sure we'll be seeing each other, with working on your grandfather's case, and everything."

"I'll call you," he said. He kissed us both good-bye on the cheek, and we told him we'd see him soon.

*   *   *

"You two are headed for *The Jerry Springer Show*," I told Sam as we walked back toward our car.

"What are you talking about?"

"I'm signing you up now for 'I Married My Cousin.' I mean, oy vay. I could've been eaten by a bear or abducted by an ax murderer and you two wouldn't have noticed."

We slid into the front seat and Sam paused before she turned the key in the ignition. "I keep thinking—this is so awful that I even think this—that a part of me doesn't even want him to be our relative, so that . . . well, because . . . " She started the car.

"Because you like him," I said.

Her face looked even more flushed than before. "Figures, with my luck. I meet a guy I like and he turns out to be related to me. And the worst thing is, I can't even tell him we're related."

"I've been thinking about that," I said, "and maybe someday we could tell them. Difriggio said there's a five-year statute of limitations for grand larceny, right? So when that's up, couldn't we tell the truth?"

"Maybe," Sam said. "I hope so. Otherwise he's going to have no idea why I'm giving him the cold shoulder forever."

6

Mackenzie set up a meeting for us with the art conservator Susan MacDonald on Sunday afternoon. Gus and Sam decided Mackenzie and I should go alone, while the two of them spent the day looking through databases and old records for any signs of Ruth Brauner, Frankie Weinstein, and a few friends of Ruth's whose names Leo had given them. They were also going to research the Art Loss Register, the largest private international database of stolen, missing, and looted works of art.

Mackenzie picked me up in her mom's blue pickup truck, and we drove to Indianapolis, to Susan MacDonald's studio.

"She's a great artist, my mom says," Mackenzie said while she drove. "She's a painter and conserves art for a living. She was a fellow at the Metropolitan Museum of Art in New York City."

Susan MacDonald's studio was in a gray stone building above an art gallery called ArtMania. A creaky old elevator opened into her huge loft, which had white walls and floor-to-ceiling windows. She greeted us at the door in jeans and a smock, her glasses askew and her tousled hair sticking up in strange places.

"Please excuse the mess here, I'm in the middle of a project. I'm restoring a Robert Wenzel sculpture," she said.

A three-foot-high black sculpture of a dancer stood in the middle of the floor. Around the room were bottles of strange liquids. A microscope sat on one of five large tables that filled the room. Paintings were laid on top of the tables. Shelved along one wall were rolls of canvas and linen, of different weaves and weights of cloth, and a strange-looking machine she called a vacuum hot table. "I use that to repair holes in the backs," she said.

The whole place smelled like chemicals. "How long have you been doing this?" I asked her.

"Over twenty years. I lived in New York for most of that time, but I missed the Midwest—I grew up here. So I decided to come back and run a regional lab. I work for Midwestern museums mostly now, and private owners and galleries."

She brewed tea for us in her makeshift kitchen, and served it in three matching mugs with Edvard Munch's *The Scream* on them. We sat on tall stools by a window and told her all about the Sebrid painting.

"Your mom's right about Dale DeCarlo. I'd like to find out the provenance of a lot of paintings he owns," she said. "His late father—he died just six months ago—he was involved in some shady European art deals as well, from what I've heard."

"What do you think we should do?" I asked her.

"Judging from the way you've described the back of the Sebrid painting, it doesn't sound like the canvas was relined. My guess is that the signature faded."

My stomach sank. "Well, then we can't prove that it's Ruth's."

She set down her mug. "Don't give up hope yet. I know that Sebrid signed some of his works with a mixture of shellac and dry pigment. Over time it's possible that the pigment faded, and the signature blended into the background. But traces might remain. There's still a way to test it."

"How?" I asked.

"Well . . . " She got down off her stool and started opening cabinets, searching for something. "You need a UV light. If the signature's there somewhere it would show up under a UV light. It will only work in the dark, though." She reached her hand deep into a shelf and pulled out what looked like a foot-long lightbulb. "Here you go."

She handed the light to me.

"But how are we going to do it?" I asked. "How could we get them to turn the lights off in the gallery so we can shine the UV light on the back?"

"Do you think the museum would let us?" Mackenzie asked.

"No way," I said. "Leo said they didn't even want to talk to him about the painting. They're not going to want to help us verify stolen Holocaust art."

Susan nodded. "The Aldredge shows great art, but they're sure not known for their friendliness and equanimity."

96

I suddenly almost regretted not going on a date with the Gnome; that would be a way back in. I doubted he'd even speak to us now, after we'd stood him up.

"I'm sorry I can't be of more help," Susan said. She gathered up our empty *Scream* mugs and put them in the sink.

We thanked her and walked back to Mackenzie's car. I sighed. "I'm going to have to sit in a corner with my Sherlock Holmes cap and pipe until I get an idea of how to do this UV-light thing in the museum." I told her about the gifts Colin had bought us in London. "Hey, didn't Sherlock Holmes play violin?" I asked. "Maybe you'll get struck with a sudden insight when you play."

She shrugged. "Except the only thoughts I usually have when I play are 'My chin hurts. My elbow hurts. I wonder what food is in the refrigerator.'"

Sam, Gus, and I ate dinner at the Petal Diner that night. Wilda had made her special chicken-fried steak; Gus devoured his piece in three bites.

"We didn't find much," Sam said. "Frankie Weinstein died of a stroke in 1996. But Leo did give us the name of the woman who ran the boardinghouse, Hester Klein, and we've got an address for her. She lives in the Bethel Rest Home in Skokie. We're hoping Hester Klein can help us get in touch with some other friends of Ruth's. Also, we looked up *Lovers in the Village* on the Art Loss Register, but it's not listed."

"We're going to have to take a trip to Chicago," Gus said.

"When are we going?" I asked.

Sam speared her peas with a fork. "You've got school, Sophie. Gus and I are going by ourselves, tomorrow."

"I can miss a couple days of school," I said.

"No, you can't," Sam said.

I glared at her. Sometimes this legal-guardian thing was incredibly annoying.

"Gus's sister lives in Chicago," Sam said. "We're going to stay with her overnight."

I took a bite of my chicken-fried steak. "I didn't know you had a sister." I pictured a female version of Gus, burly and slightly balding, in a dress. Not a pretty picture. I stifled a laugh.

Gus folded his hands on the table. "Her name's Rita."

"If you two are going to stay in Chicago, then I'm going to invite Mackenzie to sleep over. I've got some new fall-colored nail polishes from Sephora on-line I've been wanting to try anyway. We'll do homework and mud masks and paint our toenails." I tried to convince myself that I wasn't going to be missing out on anything at all. "You'll wish you had stayed home to join us."

Gus swigged his fourth cup of coffee. "Let me tell you, these were not the kinds of conversations we had on the force."

At school the next day, Colin, his friend Fred, and Mackenzie and I ate lunch under the Old Tree. We updated them on everything we'd learned about the case.

"I talked to my dad about the whole painting thing last night," Colin said. "He's a lawyer, you know, and he knows a little about art law. He said courts are usually ruling in favor of the person making the claim these days. He also said more stolen Holocaust art would probably have been returned by now, except that museums aren't making much of an effort to look into the backgrounds of works that have murky histories. Also, a lot of the claimants die before the painting's history has been traced—that generation is pretty old now."

Fred's red hair glowed in the sun. "Isn't there like a statute of limitations or something, though? I mean, that all happened a really long time ago."

"My dad told me about this one case—" Colin took out his notebook and flipped through it. "It was in New York—*Menzel* v. *List,* in 1966. The defendant, an art collector, brought up the statute of limitations, but the court decided that the statute doesn't begin until the rightful owner of the painting has been found. In a lot of cases, though, the owner's never found."

For the first time I began to wonder what the chances really were that we'd find Ruth. Maybe Gus's skepticism had been right. Was she even still alive?

"Also, if the guy who owns the painting knows that it was stolen Holocaust art, he's legally responsible," Colin said.

In mechanics class that afternoon, Chester decided to take us outside to work. For the first part of the semester we'd been studying engine parts and memorizing diagrams; we'd learned how to change oil and take apart an engine. Being the only girl in the class wasn't as fun as I'd thought. It was a little intimidating. Plus I was the only one who minded getting grease on my clothes.

Today Chester gripped his pale blue overalls and gazed at us through his impossibly thick glasses, then led us outside to the parking lot, where a gray '76 Chevy Nova was parked. The car was in such bad shape it would have made our Buick look new. The Chevy's threadbare formerly plush seats were stained with so many brown and yellow splotches they looked tie-dyed, and its dented, scratched body seemed to have survived multiple demolition derbies.

"Pete Teagarden, you get in there and try to start this thing," Chester said, and handed him the keys.

Ever since the bottle-lamb incident I was embarrassed to be around Pete. He was the star mechanic of the class—he could identify every engine part with barely a blink.

But now even Pete seemed hesitant about getting inside the hunk of metal that barely resembled a car; he looked at some of the other guys and laughed. He tried to open the driver's-side door, but it was stuck; he had to get in through the passenger side. When he turned the key in the ignition, nothing happened. The situation was strikingly similar to several experiences I'd had with our Buick.

Pete looked up helplessly at Chester.

"Yup. It's a fixer-upper," Chester said. "Now tell everyone the mileage."

Pete squinted at the odometer. "Forty-nine thousand."

Chester nodded. "Make that two hundred and forty-nine thousand—the odometer's turned over twice. In two months we're gonna get this thing up and running, just like new."

Chester launched into a long monologue about pistons, crankshafts, flywheels, and swaybar bushings. I was only half listening; I was too busy sizing up Pete again. There was something charismatic about him. He seemed like the star of a high school television show—blond and tall and the captain of the football team. I couldn't stop staring at him. Chester interrupted my daydreaming by saying, "Sophie, you know what a swaybar bushing is, don't you? Can you explain it to the class?"

Swaybar Bushing? It sounded like the name of a character in a romance novel. I had no idea what he was talking about.

"Swaybar bushing," I said uncomfortably. "Swaybar bushing is . . . " I didn't know. "Uh . . . I'm sorry. I can't remember."

Chester scratched his chin. "Maybe it was your sister I explained it to. I replaced them on your car, last time you brought it in. Swaybar bushings secure the swaybar, or stabilizer bar, preventing body leans in turns . . . "

He went on to tell us all about contact breakers, coils, distributors, rotor arms, and a hundred other things that still sounded like a foreign language to me. Then he told us to work in pairs and come up with a plan to fix this hunk of metal.

Usually when we were assigned to work in pairs I ended up being Ted Pinkerton's partner. None of the other guys wanted to be my partner, since I knew so little about cars. Ted Pinkerton wore jeans two inches too short, and sneakers covered in duct tape; no one wanted to be his partner either. I was about to sit next to Ted when I saw Pete moving toward me.

"Want to work together?" Pete asked.

"Sure." I swallowed.

He smiled. "I had no idea what a swaybar bushing was either," he told me.

We sat in the grass, writing up a plan in my notebook. I kept sneaking glances at his tanned forearms and navy blue Venice Football T-shirt.

"You look nice today," he said. I didn't look nice that day—I was wearing my worst pair of jeans since all my other ones were soaking in stain remover, to get the grease spots out. I wished I'd worn something nicer. Was he flirting with me? Maybe he'd already worked his way through every other girl at Venice High. Maybe he was another Troy, flirting with girls left and right. Good-looking but brainless. Pete seemed more sincere and smarter than Troy, though. Mackenzie had told me that Pete and her brother had coached football over the summer at a camp for kids from troubled homes in Indianapolis. And he'd gotten one of the highest scores in the junior class on his PSATs last year. I needed to ask her more about him.

"So why did your family move here from Cleveland?" he asked me.

"It's just me and my sister actually—"

"Really? Where are your folks?"

I wished someone had told him; I was so tired of talking about how my parents were dead. The strange reactions, the awkwardness.

"My parents died in a car accident," I said, giving him the usual lie.

"Oh wow. Wow."

That was a conversation damper. I stared out at the field. Why couldn't I just be a normal teenager like everybody else?

He looked at me awkwardly. He clearly didn't know what to say. "I—uh—I'm sorry," he said finally.

"Thanks. My sister and I are really close. And we've got lots of extended family, too. Even nearby, in Indiana." What was coming out of my mouth?

"That's great." He nodded.

"Yeah." I looked up at the sky. "Tons of cousins." Sam would murder me if she knew I was saying this. I didn't even know why I was saying it exactly . . . I guessed I just wanted to sound normal, for a change.

"So what are you doing Saturday night?" he asked.

My heart bounced in my chest like a rubber ball. "Saturday night?"

"Do you have plans?"

"Plans? Nooo . . . no plans."

"Nick Roxby—a middle linebacker on the team—it's his birthday, and some guys are having a party. Do you want to come with me?"

I floated the whole way home from school that day. It was clear and cool out; little puffy clouds dotted the sky over the cornfields. Nonpigeon birds swooped over-head as Mackenzie and I headed down the road. It was so nice out that we'd decided to walk into town.

"I can't believe you're going out with Pete," she said.

"We're not going out. It's just a party."

"I wish I knew more about him. I guess I only ever see him with my brother, and we don't exactly hang out

103

together, to say the least. He is cute, though. At least if things work out with you two, you can ask him to the Sadie Hawkins Dance."

"Whose dance?"

"Sadie Hawkins. They don't have that in Cleveland? It's when the girls ask the guys to go. Haven't you seen that poster at school about it?"

"Oh—I think I did. I didn't know what it was."

"It's going to be a fund-raiser for Venice and the surrounding towns. They're hoping to raise some money for Venice's Save the Canal project."

"It needs some money," I said. Flyers shouting SAVE THE CANAL! were posted throughout town, with a phone number to donate money to. Judging from the perpetual desertlike state of the canal, the organization apparently hadn't made too much progress yet.

"The theme's going to be 'Bountiful Harvest,' and get this—it's going to be a square dance, with a caller."

I'd never square-danced before. "Sounds . . . fun. I think."

"They're relying on Venice High students to sell tickets to everyone we know in town—adults and everybody. The more people who we can get to go, the better."

"Who are you going to ask?"

She shrugged. "I don't know. This is going to be a tough one."

The cornfields gave way to soybeans. "Have you ever had a boyfriend?" I asked her.

"Nope. Not a real one."

"Me neither. Unless you count a random make-out

session with Randy Chaefsky at my old school," I said.

"That's more than I've done."

"Really?" Mackenzie was so tall and beautiful, I would've thought she'd have kissed a hundred guys.

"I did kiss Kevin Foskett at spin the bottle once. He slobbered on me," she said.

"Gross. Randy Chaefsky wasn't exactly a delicate kisser either." I imitated his tongue making its lizardlike motions.

Mackenzie laughed. We walked farther down the road. She started humming.

"'Plastic Kiss?'" I asked. It was an Evil Barbie song.

She nodded. I sang the first line of it. She did the next in a deep low voice.

"Singing as we walk across the farms—all my *Little House on the Prairie* dreams have come true!" I said mockingly.

"You do look a little like Half-Pint," she said.

"Does that make Pete Almanzo? I mean Manly? I always wondered how Laura could call her husband Manly without laughing."

"You should call Pete Manly. I bet he'd like it."

We stopped at the Petal for a snack, and then I walked Mackenzie to the bus stop. We hugged good-bye in a way I hadn't hugged someone since Viv.

"I'll go home and get my stuff, and then I'll see you at your place later," she said.

When I got home, Sam had already left for Chicago. Mackenzie arrived with a copy of *Ivan Sebrid: Painter and Philosopher* and a copy of *Beauty: The New Basics*, too.

105

"The Sebrid book is my mom's. I thought you'd like it," she said.

I sat down on the sofa and leafed through it.

"'Sebrid is known for exploring the mysteries of love and loss,'" I read aloud. "'Through symbolism he sought to portray the enduring nature of love.' That's nice." I stared at the print of *Lovers in the Village*.

I thought about the photo that Leo had shown us. He and Ruth had held each other with the same passion as the lovers in the painting. I imagined him giving her all those little chocolates, carving them into shapes, and that story filtering down to Josh, who had never even met Ruth. I pictured Leo going to Barish's drugstore every afternoon for two years, hoping Ruth would come by. I wondered if romantic love was like other types of love—that even fifty years could pass and you still loved the person just as much. I'd never felt that kind of romantic love, but it seemed similar to the way I felt toward my parents and my friends. I loved my parents as much as I ever had. And I still loved Viv, even though I had no idea when I'd ever see her again.

I also felt strangely connected to Ruth . . . as if finding her would affirm my hope that despite all the horrible tragic events of the world, sometimes there could be happy endings. Was it wrong to believe that—was it because I was naive, or young? I didn't think so, and I wanted to find Ruth and reunite her with Leo and her family's painting, to prove it.

Mackenzie and I changed into our pajamas and picked out some recipes from the *Beauty* book. Using the ingredients in my kitchen, we whipped up an oatmeal face scrub to exfoliate, an avocado mask to moisturize, and an olive-oil hair treatment. With green goo on our faces and our heads wrapped in Saran Wrap, we sat on pillows on my living-room floor and painted our toenails After Hours Red.

"Pete was at my house with my brother when I got home from school, and he kept asking me questions about you. 'What's your friend Sophie's story? What's she like to do?' Blah blah blah."

"Really? He was asking about me?" My hand shook as I held the nail-polish brush and I smeared red all over my toe.

She lay back on the rug and placed cucumber slices across her eyes. "I told him you were too good for him."

"You didn't."

She lifted up a cucumber slice, peered at me, and smiled. "I did. It's true. I mean he's nice, but I think he's . . . just a little slow to mature. That's how my mom puts it at least. If you could hear him and my brother talk sometimes. 'Dude.' 'No, dude.' 'Really, dude.' 'Dude!' It's mortifying."

I wanted to ask her more, but our conversation was interrupted by a knock on the door. It was Colin.

"Sophie?" he asked. "Is that you under that layer of sludge?"

"We're beautifying," Mackenzie called from the living room.

"We only have to leave it on for ten more minutes," I said.

He was holding a Scrabble set. "Your sister told me to check in on you. She wanted me to make sure you didn't burn down the house or anything."

"Hmmph," I said. "We're fine."

He tilted the Scrabble. "Up for a game?"

We always played Lorna Scrabble, a version of the game our mom had made up. The only rule was that you had to make up fictional words from the letters you picked, then invent a plausible definition for each word; if you used a real word, you lost the game.

After Mackenzie and I washed our masks off we arranged the board on the table.

Colin went first. "Odrolly," he said as he placed his letters on the board. "The process of stealing famous works of art and stealthily covering your tracks."

"Ikywelt." I put my letters down. "A rare, gnomelike type of museum security guard, usually under five-feet tall."

It was Mackenzie's turn. "Fythmus. The gland that releases romantic hormones, which is obviously going full blast in Pete Teagarden right now," she said.

"What?" Colin asked.

"Pete Teagarden asked Sophie on a date," she said.

Colin dropped one of his squares. "Don't tell me you're actually thinking of going out with that guy."

I fiddled with my letters. "Why not?"

"I thought you learned your lesson after Troy."

"Pete's different," I said.

He sniffed.

"But you don't even know him."

Colin shook his head. "He's just not your type."

"What's my type?"

He stared at me. "Well, someone who doesn't try so

108

hard to be popular, first of all. Someone who reads . . . "

"Pete reads."

"Yeah. *Popular Mechanics* and *TV Guide*." He picked more letters out of the bag. "You need someone more complicated. More like you," he said.

"That's true," Mackenzie said. "I think Colin has a point."

"Complicated? Why do I want complicated? My life is complicated enough." And they didn't even know the half of it. I lay back on the pillow and put two cucumber slices over my eyes.

7

The next afternoon I was lying on the sofa reading *Their Eyes Were Watching God* when there was a knock on the door. I thought it might be Colin, armed with some sandwiches and more warnings about Pete. I looked through the peephole. It was Josh.

"Hi," I said, surprised to see him there.

"Hey, Sophie." He was holding a bouquet of wild-flowers. "Is Sam here?"

"No—she, uh—she actually went to Chicago—for your grandfather's case. She and Gus are doing some research there. She'll be home later, after dinner."

"Oh." He looked crestfallen. "I thought she'd be here."

"Do you want to come in?"

"Sure. Um, I brought these for Sam . . . "

I took the flowers from him. "She'll love them." I put them in a vase and then gave him a brief tour of our house.

"Nice place," he said.

"Thanks. Do you want some . . . cookies? Tea? A Yoo-

Hoo?" I almost wanted to call him Cousin Josh. That's how Wilda referred to her relatives. "I got Cousin Bill in Muncie, and Cousin Raelene in Fort Wayne . . . " Wilda would say.

"Cookies sound great."

I brought out some Oreos and we sat on the sofa.

"That was really nice of you to bring flowers."

He nodded. "I hope she likes them."

"I'm sure she will."

"Really? I mean . . . I just don't know with her. Sometimes I think she likes me, but then . . . it's like she's holding back or something." He shrugged. "I don't know."

"That's because she's your cousin," I wanted to say. I wondered if they made a Hallmark card for the occasion: "I'd like you if we weren't related!"

I picked up another Oreo. "Sam's just . . . complicated." At least Colin would think that was a good thing.

"She seems like it," he said, with a laugh. He stared around our living room, soaking it all in. "You know . . . I've been thinking of asking her on a real date. Like out to dinner or something. You think she'd say yes?"

"Yeah—yeah, I'm sure she would." Well, I wasn't exactly sure. But I could convince her to go. Since she'd never even been on a real date before, maybe having her first one with her cousin would be a good way to ease into the whole thing. Also, she could find out more information then about Josh's branch of the Shattenberg family. And considering Sam had encouraged me to go on that investigative date with Troy this summer, I figured it was her turn now.

111

He smiled, and sank back into the couch, looking relieved. "I'm glad I stopped by. Thanks, Sophie."

"How's your grandfather?" I asked.

"He's okay. He's really hoping you guys find Ruth. After all these years . . . I hope it's possible."

"I'm sure it is. We'll do our best, I promise."

"Well." He stood up. "I guess I should get back."

"I'll tell Sam you stopped by."

We hugged each other good-bye, and I watched him get inside his car and drive off.

Sam trudged up the porch steps at ten o'clock that night. "How did we ever live in New York?" she asked. "Chicago's traffic, the dirt, the noise . . . it drove me crazy. I don't know how we did it."

"You sound like a suburban housewife," I said, helping her carry her suitcase. "So what was it like?"

"It's sort of like New York but a little smaller. Not as condensed. They have a subway but they call it 'the El' and the city's right on Lake Michigan, which looks a lot cleaner than the East River."

"Does Gus's sister look like him?"

"Nothing like him. She's really tall and skinny, and she's this high-powered lawyer. She wore a fancy business suit, and her apartment is spotless. I asked Gus if he was adopted. Rita said she used to ask their parents the same thing. She can't wait to meet you, by the way." She sat down on the couch and started untying her sneakers.

"I can't wait to meet her either. So what'd you find out?"

"We tracked down Hester Klein. She's ninety-two years old and stuck in this depressing nursing home. She didn't remember Ruth Brauner at all—or much of anything, really—but she did have a dim recollection of a friend of Ruth's named Elsie Schenker. She said Elsie married a man named Goldfarb. So we looked up Elsie Goldfarb and got an address for her—but she wasn't around. We left our card with one of the neighbors and told them to have Elsie contact us. If she doesn't, I think we're going to have to make a return trip to Chicago sometime."

She got herself a glass of water. "We also did some more database and public-records searches there. Nothing for Ruth came up on the Social Security Master Death Index, driving and voting records, old obituaries, or marriage licenses. Nothing. So there's a real chance she's alive—that's the good news. Gus thinks if she was dead it would've come up under her Social Security number or date of birth somewhere. Unless . . . "

"Unless what?"

"Unless she somehow got a new Social Security number . . . like we did." She shrugged. "I don't know. It's weird. She's completely off the books."

I pictured the pretty girl from Leo's photo changing her identity like we had. Why would she have needed to?

Sam noticed the flowers on the coffee table. "Where'd you get those?"

"I didn't get them. Someone came by and left them for you."

She dropped one of her sneakers with a thud. "Josh?" she whispered.

"Yup, Cousin Josh. He likes you."

Her face lit up. "This is the first time anyone's ever given me flowers." She touched the leaves.

"That's not the only thing he wants to give you," I said under my breath.

"What?"

"He wants to ask you out on a date. He told me he's going to—he asked if I thought you'd go."

"What did you say?" Her voice was as high as a choirboy's.

"I said yes." I explained my plan to her, how she'd go on this date and casually bring up all our are-you-my-relative questions.

"I'm not going on a date with him. I can't. I'm just . . . I don't know how to be on a date, cousin or no cousin. I can't go."

"Yes, you can."

"No, I can't. Not unless you come with me."

Colin stood in the back of his shop, greasing a bike chain. "Wait—you want me to do what?"

"Go to dinner with me so it looks natural that I'm at the same restaurant as Sam and Josh. We're going to pretend we just met up there by coincidence."

"Have you been watching *I Love Lucy* marathons again?" He wiped his hands on a rag.

"Just a couple episodes."

He examined the wheel of a bright red Schwinn. It looked similar to the one he'd sold to Sam and me when we first came to town. "Why don't you ask Pete to go with you?" he asked.

114

"I can't ask Pete to do this. I don't even know him. Besides, he'd think I was crazy."

"And I already know you're crazy." Colin grinned.

"So are you. That's why we get along so well."

"And if Pete went you couldn't use any words longer than two syllables."

"Pete did really well on his PSATs," I said.

"Oh please. Since when do PSATs measure intelligence? How do you think Sartre would've done on the PSATs?"

"I bet he would've done great. Especially on the Critical Reading section." I looked through a box of dusty old books on the floor. "Please come with me. The only way Sam will go on the first date of her life is if I'm willing to go with her, and give her advice in the bathroom. My sister's entire romantic life is at stake here." I needed to up the romantic angle since I couldn't tell Colin about the cousin issue.

Colin leaned against a bookshelf. "Okay. I'll go. I wouldn't want to sabotage Sam's entire romantic future."

"Really? You'll come?"

"Yes. Really."

I hugged him, and we made plans to meet at his place and drive to the restaurant. "So what makes you the dating expert?" he asked.

I shrugged. "Well, I read a lot of magazines. Just the other day I bought a *Cosmo* that was dedicated to the art of flirting and dating."

"That would do it." He smiled his lopsided grin.

* * *

115

For the first dinner date of her life my sister wore our mother's black silk blouse and wool skirt, and a pair of my high-heeled boots. Josh took her jacket from her and hung it up on a hook—very chivalrous. I kept sneaking looks at them as they were seated. Colin and I sat five tables away, behind three potted palms.

Sam glanced between the trees, checking that we were there. Josh hadn't seen us yet. The plan was for her to get up from her seat, walk by my table, and act surprised that Colin and I were there, too.

"We should probably start practicing our 'Oh my Gods!', don't you think? So we sound authentically surprised? OMIGOD!" Colin mocked in his best fake-cheerleader voice.

"Oh, be quiet. Look—she's getting up from her table. She's walking over."

"Oh my God!" Sam said, when she reached our table. "Funny to see you two here!"

"What a surprise!" I said.

"I'm shocked," Colin said.

Josh peered around the palm trees, and started walking toward us. "Your sister's here, too?"

"I thought you told me you were coming here tomorrow night," I said to Sam. "When you mentioned this restaurant Colin and I had to try it. I didn't realize you were here tonight. I must be all mixed up."

"All mixed up," Colin echoed.

"Well—it's great to see you," Josh said. "Do you want to join us at our table?"

"Oh . . . no thanks," I said. I thought Sam would have the best luck with her questions on her own. "We—um, we wanted to be alone."

"I didn't realize you two were a couple," Josh said with a smirk.

"Sophie and I love French food. Don't we, honey?" Colin said.

"Yes, honey. We do. It's our favorite."

"Well—we'll leave you two alone," Josh said, still smirking, and walked back to his table.

"So what did this magazine article which qualifies you to be a dating expert say?" Colin asked me. "I'm eager to know."

"Well, you're supposed to laugh at everything the guy says. Make lots of eye contact." I looked up at the ceiling. "What else? Oh—if their pupils dilate that's a good thing. And if the guy really likes you, he'll offer to pay for your dinner."

"Interesting," Colin said as he perused the menu. "Are my pupils dilated?"

"Your eyes are dark brown. I can't tell." I smiled.

I looked over at Sam; she scratched her ear twice— our signal to meet in the bathroom. "Conference time," I told Colin, and got up from my seat.

By the bathroom mirror she let out a huge, deep sigh. "Do I look fat in this skirt? I think Mommy was a lot skinnier than me. These heels are killing me. How do you walk in these things?"

"They're not so bad—those are my low ones," I said.

"He keeps asking me all these questions. What do I say? All about our family, blah blah blah . . . I'm lying my head off. All about Cleveland. I keep trying to turn the conversation back to him, but he says he wants to talk about me, to get to know me."

I fixed a smudge of her eye shadow and gave her a fresh coat of lip gloss. Sam almost never wore makeup; she winced as I applied it. "Did you ask him about his family?"

"I haven't even had a chance," she said.

"*Cosmo* didn't say anything about how to hide your identity on a date. But you're good at sticking to our story. Just . . . try talking about Leo. A third party—that's always good."

"Okay. Leo. You don't think this lipstick is too shiny? I can't believe you made me wear lipstick."

"It's gloss, it's supposed to be shiny. You look beautiful," I said, standing back to survey my handiwork.

The rest of the evening passed quickly—Colin ordered *boeuf aux pommes frites* in a quick spatter of expert French. "What?" I asked him.

"Steak and fries," he said. I ordered the same thing. I kept glancing over at Sam, but she seemed to be doing okay.

"You know, I've been thinking about this whole signature-on-the-back-of-the-painting thing, and I've got an idea," Colin said. I'd told him all about our meeting with Susan MacDonald after Mackenzie and I'd gotten back from Indianapolis.

"What?"

"I think we should break into the museum."

"*What?* How would we break into a museum?" Visions of *Mission Impossible*–like maneuvers swam through my head.

"Well—it was pretty easy to take a glance at the back

118

of the painting. Security seems pretty low-key at the Aldredge, so I don't think we'd get caught. And remember that Bruce Busby exhibit we saw? There was an opening in the side of that tent which I bet we could crawl into and wait until the museum closed."

"Kind of like *From the Mixed-up Files of Mrs. Basil E. Frankweiler,*" I said. I loved that book—it was about a brother and sister who run away from home and hide out in the Metropolitan Museum.

"Exactly. That's one of my favorite books." He beamed.

"What about Sam and Gus, though? Gus will flip out . . . and I'm sure Sam would want to be in on it," I said.

"I've thought about it, and I think just you and I should do it because if we did get caught, we're juveniles. We can just pretend it was a prank or something, spending the night in a Bruce Busby sculpture. They couldn't really do anything to us, whereas with your sister being twenty-one . . . she could really get in trouble."

"True."

He put his napkin on the table. "We'd need a camera with high-speed film, though, to get proof of the signature. I bet Fred could help us. He took photography last year and Mr. Benson still lets him borrow equipment sometimes. He borrowed a tripod and camera last month, just to photograph his dog Herman."

"It sounds like a good plan," I said. "Of course first we need to find Ruth. It's not worth it to take the risk if we don't know for certain that Ruth wants it back."

"Good point." The check came; Colin snatched it

before I could.

"What are you doing?" I asked.

"Nothing." He put money in the folder and handed it right to the waiter.

I rested my hands on the table. "I was going to pay for dinner," I said. "You're my accomplice." I should have known Colin was too generous to let me pay.

He ignored me. "Well, we don't have to mention the idea of breaking in to anyone till Ruth's found."

I nodded. I wondered how Sam would react to the idea. I watched as she and Josh put on their jackets.

"Looks like a successful date," Colin said. "She seems to be doing all right on her own."

Josh and Sam waved good-bye to us, and left the restaurant a few minutes before we did. When Colin and I pulled up to the house we saw Josh give my sister a good-night kiss. It looked like he was aiming for her mouth, but she turned quickly and gave him her cheek. Then she hugged him and ran inside.

"Thanks for dinner," I told Colin.

He leaned on the steering wheel. "Thank you."

"Good night." I smiled.

"Good night, Sophie."

I kissed him on the cheek. Inside the house I found Sam pacing across the living-room floor. She'd already taken off her boots and had my shark slippers on.

"You're not going to believe what he just told me," she said.

"What?"

Her eyes glowed. "I got on the subject of family trees—I told him I'd studied genealogy in college, and

Josh said they did have distant cousins named David and Solomon."

For a second, I could barely breathe.

She put her hands to her head. "Oh God, what am I doing?" she said. "My cousin just kissed me!"

"It was on the cheek," I said. "I saw from the car. The cheek doesn't count."

She kept pacing.

"So we really are related." I sat down on the couch and hugged my knees to my chest.

"The thing is, I like him," Sam said.

"Well. It's not so bad. I looked it up on the Internet and I think it's only illegal to marry your first cousin."

She stopped in her tracks. "Great. That's really good to know," she said, and then bopped me with a couch pillow.

8

On Friday morning we went to see Difriggio. We wanted to ask him how to handle our new-relatives situation, and to see if he knew anything about DeCarlo. I left school early, and Sam and I drove to Indianapolis. We told Gus that we were going shopping and running errands in Indianapolis after school. He was going to meet us there later to talk to DeCarlo, who was going to be at an auction house in the city that evening.

Difriggio's office was in a red-brick building above a pizza/tattoo/pool parlor in the seedy part of town. We walked down the back hallway to the private elevator, which had letters instead of numbers on the buttons, and pressed *S* for his office. As soon as we stepped out of the elevator we realized we were in trouble.

A man in a black hat and gray suit stood with his back to us, talking to Difriggio. Difriggio caught sight of us out of the corner of his eye—his fingers drummed the wall and his furry eyebrows wiggled furiously, like dancing ferrets. Sam grabbed my hand and yanked me down the hall, out of sight.

I started trembling. Difriggio had looked closer to scared than I'd ever seen him look before. Their voices started coming closer. Difriggio said loudly, "Yeah, I'll let you know if I hear anything about the Shattenbergs. Thanks for your card, Mr. Hertznick."

We waited till we heard the elevator ping and Difriggio say even more loudly, "Good-bye, Mr. Hertznick." A few moments later he said in a thin voice, "Okay, girls, you can come out now."

We padded around the corner, and as soon as Difriggio saw us he started yelling. "Whatta ya, CRAZY, coming here NOW? Didn't ya get my MESSAGE?!"

Apparently anger brought out his Brooklyn accent.

"No," Sam said meekly. "What message?"

"On ya CELL! As soon as Hertznick showed up I paged my assistant Artie and he called your phone and warned you two not to come till Hertznick was gone! I don't believe this. That was too close." He took off his Yankees cap and ran his fingers through his thick hair.

Sam took the cell phone out of her shoulder bag. "We must've been out of range when he called—there's a message, but I didn't get it. Who's Hertznick?"

"You gotta check that thing all the time! Before you leave today, I'm getting you a pager, too. You can keep that on always. And Hertznick—let's go into my office." He mumbled something in Italian.

Difriggio sat down at his polished mahogany desk. Cubby, his massive orange tabby cat, jumped on his lap and stretched her paws across his knees. Difriggio didn't fit the stereotype of a master criminal—for one thing, he displayed copies of *Cat Fancy* around his office.

"Enid Gutmyre hired a PI to look for you. Hal Hertznick—I've heard his name before. He's good. He's got connections," he said.

I felt light-headed and suddenly sick.

"How did he track us here?" Sam asked. Her face was as white as a marshmallow.

"He interviewed kids at Bronx Science and LaGuardia," Difriggio said. "And someone pointed him in the direction of Felix—heard that Felix was in the fake-ID business—and someone else knew that Felix had connections to me. So, he tracked me here, and is sniffing around Indy a little bit. But he's got nothing on you yet. He's just checking out leads—and we better keep it that way."

"I can't believe he's here," Sam said. "Do you think he'll come to Venice?"

Difriggio shook his head. "I think I'm the only lead he had—he waited in Indy for three days till I got back in town." He scratched Cubby behind her ears. "If he had a lead to Venice, he would've gone there in the meantime. I don't think he's got any way to track you there. Don't worry about that yet. But for the time being be extra careful. Watch your backs. And check your messages! I can't help you girls if you get careless."

He buzzed Artie and asked him to bring up a pager.

The skin on my neck prickled at the thought of being so close to getting caught. The idea of Hertznick hanging around Indianapolis . . . it couldn't have been much worse.

"What should we do now?" Sam asked him. "Is he going to come back?"

Difriggio glanced at his watch. "I don't think so. I'm having Hertznick trailed to see where he's headed. You should stay here till we're sure he's far out of town. We've gotta talk about planting some fake leads to throw Hertznick off course. I'm thinking we'll have an e-mail sent from you to one of your friends, from a false location."

"That won't bring him closer to us?" Sam asked.

"Not if we do it right," Difriggio said.

"Can we send something to my friend Vivien? I mean, if we're going to send something made up, can we send it to her?"

Difriggio nodded. Cubby rolled over on his lap, and he rubbed her belly. "I think that would be all right."

"We had a couple questions for you, too." Sam told him about Leo.

Difriggio nodded, absorbing the information. "It's an interesting situation. Don't mention anything to him yet, though. It's still not clear if you're related, even if his grandson told you some relatives have the same names. It's always safer to be careful, not to give your hand away until you have no choice. Until you're sure they're on your side. But in the meantime, you can feel him out, see how much you trust the two of them. Just be careful not to let anything slip."

"We're careful," Sam said. "Very careful."

"Once it's proven—if it's proven—then what do we do?" I asked Difriggio. "Can we tell them who we are?"

Difriggio scratched Cubby on the sides of her face. She purred like an electric drill. "I think we should take this step by step. Let's see if we can get more information, some proof, before we make any decisions," he said.

We told Difriggio about Dale DeCarlo. Difriggio's whole face darkened. "Hertznick, Dale DeCarlo . . . you girls seem to be attracting trouble," Difriggio said, shaking his head.

"We're supposed to meet Gus at an auction house and talk to DeCarlo tonight," Sam told him.

"You two just hang back and let Gus do the questioning," Difriggio said. "DeCarlo's bad news."

We stayed at Difriggio's for three hours. I couldn't even eat anything, I was so unnerved from the near run-in with Hertznick. It was hard to focus on writing to Viv, but with Difriggio's help I drafted an e-mail that would be sent from a contact of Difriggio's in Mexico. The e-mail said:

-----Original Message-----
From: love4shoes718@hotmail.com [Sophie Shattenberg]
To: princessofQueens1989@hotmail.com [Vivien Chun]
Sent: Wednesday September 15, 2003 1:50 A.M.
Subject: checking in

Viv!
Just wanted to let you know we're alive and ok. I can't
tell you where we are but I wanted to tell you I miss you
like crazy and I love you. Please don't tell anyone I
contacted you—even Sam doesn't know. Don't forget about
me. I know we'll see each other again someday soon.
Love,
SS

The thought that Viv would get this e-mail—even though it would be sent through Mexico and Difriggio's contacts there and probably through several other channels so it couldn't be traced back to us—the idea that she would hear from me at all, and know that I hadn't forgotten her, made me feel a little better.

After I typed the e-mail, Sam and I tried to distract ourselves from our raging nerves. We played with Cubby, scratching her massive stomach and throwing her catnip mouse around Difriggio's conference room, which calmed us down a tiny bit, but not much. I hadn't felt this shaken up since the night we'd left Queens.

Finally Difriggio called us into his office and told us that Hertznick had been trailed all the way to Fort Wayne, which was two and a half hours away. He wouldn't be back anytime soon, and Difriggio was going to try to keep track of Hertznick as best he could. Sam and I said good-bye to Difriggio, and that we'd talk to him later. We promised we'd be more careful.

"Just when it seemed like we were really fitting in," Sam said as we got back into our car. "Just when we're settled in Venice and we don't want to leave, here comes Enid's henchman." She sounded so defeated.

"He's not going to find us," I said. "There's no way. How could he track us to Venice? There are so many little towns all over Indiana—it would take him forever to visit each one."

"Let's hope he doesn't." She started the car.

"I wish we could just tell someone our story. Either Gus . . . or Leo. Or Colin. Then they could watch out for us, too. I mean, do you think they would turn us in?"

"I don't think so," she said. "But it's still a risk we can't afford to take right now."

We met Gus at the Maxwell Auction House. He was wearing a dark gray suit that was a size too small.

"You look nice," Sam said. Her voice was quiet. I stood closely beside her and stared at my feet.

"What's with you two?" Gus asked. "You look like someone just died."

"Mackenzie's pet ferret, Wiggles, died," I said, thinking of Difriggio's furry, ferretlike eyebrows. I wanted to explain our moroseness without giving anything away. "He just keeled over. Heart attack. He was young. Before his time, really."

"That's sad," Gus said dryly. "I got us all tickets for the auction." We took a seat in a back row. He held a paddle with the number 59 on it.

"Have you ever been to an auction before?" Sam asked Gus.

"Yeah, I go every week," Gus deadpanned. He motioned toward a dark figure across the room. "There he is. That's Dale DeCarlo."

DeCarlo wore a perfectly tailored black suit. He stood near the front row, talking to a group of men. His long gray hair was slicked back into a ponytail.

The auctioneer stepped to the podium and asked everyone to be seated.

"Let's see what we got here," Gus said, leafing through the auction catalog. "Yep, just what I thought. A bunch of junk I've never heard of."

They were selling paintings, drawings, and sculptures.

Some of the artists' names sounded familiar, from all the art books my mom used to have around the house. I would've been more excited to be there, except that the afternoon's events made me want to go home and hide under the covers.

The auction began; the auctioneer described each work of art for sale and began the bidding. Once, at the start of a bid, Gus stuck his paddle up.

"What are you doing?" Sam whispered.

"I'm fitting in," he murmured. Thankfully the bidding continued. Several of the paintings were owned by DeCarlo; the bids for some went up to several hundred thousand dollars.

"Wonder how many of these were stolen," Gus muttered under his breath.

After an hour, the auctioneer closed the first segment of the auction and announced that cocktails could be purchased in the hall. Gus told us to stay put while he talked to DeCarlo.

Gus walked over to a corner of the bar where DeCarlo stood talking to several men. Sam and I stepped up to the bar and ordered two orange juices. We hovered there, listening.

"Excuse me, Mr. DeCarlo. I'd like to talk to you about *Lovers in a Village.*"

DeCarlo eyed Gus up and down. "Excuse me," he said to the other men standing around him. The men walked away, and DeCarlo asked Gus, "Are you here for the auction?"

"Yes, I am."

DeCarlo's eyes slid over Gus's wrinkled, ill-fitting

suit, his ketchup-stained tie, and mismatched socks.

"Are you sure you're in the right place?" DeCarlo asked. "This isn't a flea market, my friend."

"I'd like to know the ownership history of *Lovers in a Village*," Gus said. "I'd like to know where you got that painting from."

DeCarlo's eyes narrowed. "What are you insinuating? That painting has been in my family for decades. And I assure you that from the beginning it was a bona fide purchase."

"Are you familiar with the name Ruth Brauner?"

DeCarlo's lips formed a thin hard line. "I don't know who you're talking about." He gave Gus a slithery, condescending gaze. "Excuse me, I have some legitimate buyers to conduct business with." He turned away.

"Work stolen during the Holocaust should be returned to its rightful owners," Gus said loudly. People turned and stared. A woman took a few steps away from Gus.

DeCarlo didn't even turn around, he just walked back into the auction room. Gus ambled over to us.

"Gus," I said. "That was heroic."

"I was going to take a more friendly approach, to get him to talk more, but he's such a . . . " He closed his mouth and leaned against the bar. "I guess I lost it a little there. Just wanted to let that guy have it."

"I'm glad you did," Sam said. "He deserved it."

Gus ordered a gin and tonic. "I'd bet the price of that painting that it wasn't a 'bona fide purchase.' "

At home that night Sam and I lay on the couch, trying to

130

quell the uneasiness in our stomachs from the run-in with Hertznick with a couple episodes of *A Makeover Story.* (My suggestion—thankfully *Wall $treet Week* wasn't on.)

The phone rang. We both jumped.

"You get it," I said.

"No, I don't think we should answer it," she said.

I knew she was thinking what I was: it might be Enid's PI.

"Let the machine pick up," I said.

"Sophie? Hi, this is Pete. I, uh . . . didn't see you in mechanics today, so I just wanted to make plans for tomorrow night."

"Oh my God, the date," I said.

"What date? Who's Pete?" Sam asked.

I snatched up the cordless phone.

"Hi, Pete—it's Sophie."

"Oh. Hi. Are you sick or something?"

"Sick?"

"Well, you weren't in mechanics class—and you sound kinda funny."

"Yeah, I'm not really feeling that well today."

That was the truth. I walked into the bathroom with the phone and stared at myself in the mirror. My skin looked pale and I had dark circles under my eyes. I looked like I hadn't slept in three days.

"You still up for the party tomorrow night?"

"Tomorrow? Um, okay," I said. All of a sudden I wasn't so excited about going out with him. There was so much to think about with the case. And the run-in with Hertznick had triggered all these thoughts of leaving

Venice, our new friends and our new home. I wasn't ready to start all over again. But I knew it would do me good to get out of the house, to get my mind off everything.

"Uh, cool. I was thinking we could go have dinner first, and then go out to the party," he said.

"That sounds good."

"Do you like Chinese food?" he asked.

"I love it."

"Great. I'll pick you up at seven. I know the perfect place," he said, and I gave him my address.

I went into Gus's office with Sam early the next morning. We wanted to look for information about Hal Hertznick on Gus's databases. It was 8 a.m. on a Saturday, so Gus was at home fast asleep.

Before we even turned on the computer, the phone rang.

"Hello?" I asked.

Silence.

"Hello?" Sam picked up Gus's line.

"I know who you are," a deep voice growled. *"Stay away, or there's going to be trouble!"*

The line went dead.

I dropped the phone. "What was that?" My skin was covered in goose bumps. "*Who* was that? Was that Hertznick? Did he track us here?"

Sam's voice was shaky. "It couldn't be. He wouldn't call if he knew where we were—he'd show up in person, don't you think? And he wouldn't be warning us to stay away."

"Maybe it's DeCarlo?" I asked.

"Maybe," Sam said. She called Gus at home, woke him up, and told him what had just happened.

"Did you get the number?" Gus's voice crackled.

"No. It's unlisted," Sam said. "Caller ID blocked. There were a bunch of unlisted calls on the Caller ID when we came in, though," she said. "And no messages. Maybe he tried to call a few times and this was the first time he got through."

"I bet it's DeCarlo," Gus grumbled. "I'm gonna call a friend in Indy and see if he can get me some phone-tracing equipment in case the bozo calls again."

"You think he'll call again?"

"I hope so," Gus said. "So we can get him."

We left Gus's office and drove back home. "If it was DeCarlo, or someone working for him calling us, then maybe that's a good sign," Sam said in the car.

"How could a threatening call be a good sign?" I asked, taking a bite out of a chocolate doughnut. We'd made a detour by Joy-Ann Donuts and picked up a box so we could smother our nerves with sugar.

"Well—he'd only call if he had something to hide—if he didn't want us to find Ruth." She reached for a Boston crème.

"Which means maybe he knows that Ruth is alive." This was good news.

A few minutes after we stepped into our house, the phone rang. We jumped again.

"This is getting ridiculous," Sam said. "We're afraid of the stupid phone. I'm picking it up."

She touched it gingerly, as if it might explode in her

133

hands. "Hello?" Her voice was thin.

I waited.

"Oh hi, Josh." Her shoulders relaxed and she took the cordless up to her room. A few minutes later she came back downstairs and said, "I've got a date tonight, too."

"Really? We've never had dates on the same night before."

"That's because we've almost never had any dates before, ever," she said. "And technically, mine isn't actually a date, since it's with my cousin."

"Good point," I conceded. This was the second pseudodate of Sam's life, and my first real one, since I didn't count the one with Troy over the summer.

"What are you going to wear?" I asked.

She groaned. "I've got to come up with another nice outfit?" We went up to her room to look through the clothes in her closet. She threw a corduroy skirt onto a chair.

I flopped onto her bed. "You know Monday's Yom Kippur." It was fitting that all this trauma—Enid's PI and DeCarlo, and these emotions over Leo and Josh—was happening during the High Holidays, the holiest days of the year, when you were supposed to be thinking about your past and getting ready to start over.

"We should go to temple," I said. Part of Yom Kippur was the Yizkor memorial service, a special prayer service for people who'd had someone close to them die. I wanted to say the prayer for my dad, and have his name read aloud in synagogue, which was the tradition for loved ones who'd died in the previous year. We'd done it for my mom. All of this pretending not to be Jewish was really getting to me. I wanted to be myself again. "Will you ask Josh if we can go to services with him?" I asked.

"Are you kidding me? What am I going to say to him? 'How 'bout that Yom Kippur—sure sounds like fun! My sister and I'd love to fast all day and sit in the temple listening to Hebrew prayers we don't understand." Fasting was a major part of the holiday. Sam and our dad always fasted on Yom Kippur, and though I always attempted it, sometimes I only made it until three before I succumbed to a Coke and a cookie.

"I'm sure you can come up with some way to snag us an invite. Daddy'd want us to have his name read at the service. You know he would," I said.

"Then Josh and Leo would hear the name Shattenberg," she said.

"We could just put in his first name."

Her voice softened. "Maybe," she said.

9

Sam and I got ready for our dates, but without the enthusiasm we would've had just a few days before, thanks to all my worrying about Hertznick. I barely even had the energy to do my hair or put on makeup; all I did was apply a few halfhearted strokes of mascara. We were both ready early, and we sat on the couch like two old spinsters, jaded from decades of dating.

"What if Pete takes me to another town? Do you think we could run into Hertznick?" I asked her.

"Let's try not to think about it tonight," she said. Still, she jumped every time a door creaked or the wind gusted through the windows.

Josh was supposed to arrive at seven; at six forty-five, there was a knock on the door.

"He's early," I said. "There's another Shattenberg trait." Our dad would make us show up to movies forty-five minutes before they started. We always made him get us candy to alleviate our boredom. I'd probably consumed more Milk Duds and Sno-Caps than any other girl in Queens.

Sam looked through the peephole. "It's not him. It's Colin." She opened the door; Colin breezed in with a pizza and two pints of Ben & Jerry's. "Hey—I got half green-pepper-and-olive, your favorite, Sam, and half spinach-and-mushroom, for you, Soph. Why do you have your jacket on?"

I hadn't told Colin my date with Pete was tonight, to avoid getting any flak about it. "I, uh, I'm going out, and Sam has a date with Josh."

"Oh." He gazed at me. He'd surprised us with pizza before—usually you could count on Sam and me to be reading, playing Scrabble, or watching movies at home on weekend nights. "So what, are you going with her again? Going to sit at another table by yourself? Or do you want me to come, too?" he asked, grinning.

"Didn't Sophie tell you about her hot date?" Sam asked.

His grin faded. "I didn't know that was tonight." He put the pizza down on the table.

I felt terrible, all of a sudden. The mood I was in, I would rather have just hung out with Colin, eaten pizza, and rented a movie. We could've watched Audrey Hepburn and Peter O'Toole break into a museum together in *How to Steal a Million*.

"I don't even really feel like going," I said. I went into the kitchen to get spoons, and listened to Colin and my sister talking.

"Why is she going out with him?" Colin asked Sam. "He's a meathead."

"Well you know Sophie's taste in guys—*Troy*," she said.

"She really can pick 'em," Colin said as I walked back into the room.

I decided I'd ignore the comment. He didn't even know Pete. I devoured a huge bite of Phish Food ice cream and then the doorbell rang again. This time it was Josh. "Great to see you again," Josh said to Colin.

Josh had brought a bouquet of white roses with lavender for Sam. She blushed and went into the kitchen to put them in a vase. He looked at the pizza on the table, then at Colin and me, sitting on the couch. "You two staying in for a romantic evening at home?"

I'd forgotten that Josh thought Colin and I were a couple. "Oh—" I looked at the pizza and didn't feel like explaining. "Yup," I said, hoping Colin wouldn't say anything.

Sam gathered her jacket and the purse she was borrowing from me and waved good-bye. She and Josh hurried off, leaving me and Colin alone.

"So when's the meathead supposed to show?" Colin asked.

"Around now," I said. "And he's not a meathead. He did really well on—"

"The PSATs." Colin nodded. "How could I forget."

He got up to go, taking the pizza with him. I felt bad. "Maybe—I'll come by your shop if I get home early?" I said.

He shrugged. "Sure." He opened the door. Pete was standing there, about to ring the buzzer.

Colin stuck his hand out. "Oh hi. Good to see you."

"Hi," Pete said, confused. He gave me a quizzical, what's-he-doing-here look, and strolled in.

"So . . . what's the plan for this evening?" Colin asked him.

"We're, uh, going to go to dinner, and then go to Roxby's party, down by Fall's Creek Road?"

"Oh, that party," Colin said, though I had a feeling he hadn't heard of it. "Football party?"

"Some of the guys from the team are throwing it, in Hammond's Field."

"Oh yeah. Well, have fun now you two." Colin patted Pete on the back as he walked out the door.

Pete stuck his hands into the pockets of his red football jacket. "So you guys are . . . good friends?"

"Yeah," I said. I thought I should change the subject. "Where are we going to eat?"

We walked out onto the porch. "It's a surprise," he said.

Jade Palace was the only Chinese restaurant within thirty miles of Venice. It was in a converted International House of Pancakes that had been painted pink and green. The menu featured the conventional Chinese restaurant staples—moo shoo, General Tso's chicken, egg rolls, wonton soup—alongside burgers and french fries. Not a good sign.

"This place has fine cuisine," Pete said. "I think you'll be impressed. Mexican food is my favorite, but there aren't any places nearby that meet my standards." As far as I knew, Taco Bell was the closest thing to a Mexican restaurant for miles.

We settled into a booth the color of Pepto-Bismol. "Actually—if you don't mind, I'd like to order for you," he said.

"Okay." Maybe he knew some specials they made that weren't on the menu.

The waitress came over. She had bleached blond hair and eyebrows that were penciled in. There wasn't a Chinese person in sight.

"We'd like two egg-drop soups, two egg rolls, and the mademoiselle and I will share an order of lo mean noodles, kung payo shrimp, and General Teeso's chicken."

Teeso? Payo? Lo mean? "I think it's a silent T," I said.

"You want tea?"

"No—in General Tso's? The T is silent."

He laughed. "I don't think so."

Our egg rolls arrived—they were filled with frozen peas and carrots—and Pete launched into a play-by-play of the highlights of his Venice High football career. "Then I dropped back to pass on the twenty-yard line . . . and the blitz was on, so I had to scramble . . . then I threw on the run to my wide receiver, who caught it on the two-yard line and fell into the end zone for the winning touchdown."

I knew nothing about football; it was like listening to ancient Greek. "Wow." I tried to feign interest. "Really?"

"I can't believe you haven't been to any of our games. You've got to come. I promise I won't set any bottle lambs on you."

"Huh." I tried to laugh. "Good."

"You feeling okay?" he asked me. "You usually seem a lot cheerier, in mechanics class."

"I just . . . I've had one of those weeks."

"That's too bad. Did I tell you about the plays we've got planned for Homecoming?" His blue eyes darkened and lightened as he rambled on in more footballese. He was alarmingly handsome. And I did still feel attracted to him, that same sort of chemical whir I'd felt that first time I saw him in class. But with everything that had happened lately, I wanted to talk about real things. I wished I was with Colin or Mackenzie tonight. With them I wouldn't even have to say anything and they'd have a sense of what I was feeling. Maybe they didn't know exactly who I was—that I was really Sophie Shattenberg from Sunnyside, Queens—but they still knew me.

Jade Palace was the worst Chinese food I'd ever had in my life. The General "Teeso's" chicken tasted like a Stouffer's frozen entrée.

"I love this place," Pete said. "I really go for exotic cuisine, you know?"

Exotic? "They have really good Chinese food in . . . Cleveland," I said.

"I'd like to go see Cleveland sometime. I'd like to check out a big city like that. You know what my biggest dream is?"

"What?"

"Someday—I mean, after I'm in the NFL—I want to be a chef."

I was surprised he didn't pronounce it *chief*.

"I want to own my own restaurant," he said.

"Maybe you could find an old KFC to convert," I joked. "Like this Pizza Hut."

He didn't think that was funny. "I have a secret dish I'm going to make," he said.

"Really? What kind of food?"

"I need to keep it hush-hush, 'cause I don't want, like, some other chef to find out and steal it from me. But, dude. This idea is so good. Can you keep a secret? You promise you won't let it slip?"

"I promise."

"Okay. Here goes. You know that saying 'a riddle wrapped in a mystery inside an enigma'?"

I nodded.

"Well—I'm going to make the food version." He could barely sit still, he was so excited by his idea. He motioned with his hands as he spoke. "I'm going to take an enchilada, wrap it in a burrito, stick it in a taco, and serve it inside a tostada. I'm going to call it 'The Conundrum.'"

It actually sounded sort of appealing, in a bizarre way. "Interesting," I said.

"I'll have to make it for you sometime." He tilted his head and gazed at me. "You know, you and your sister have a sort of ethnic look to you. I like that."

Ethnic? I blinked at him. She can really pick 'em, Colin had said. He was probably right.

Our fortune cookies arrived. Mine didn't even have a fortune inside—this seemed like an extra bad sign.

"I really . . . should go home," I said.

"You can't go home yet. We've got to scoop the loop and then hit the party."

"Scoop the loop? What's that?"

"Scoop the loop—you know, cruise the main drag of town? It's fun."

I thought I'd seen something about "cruising" in a teen movie once, but I didn't know people did it for real. "I don't think so. You know, I'm kind of tired," I said.

"Oh, come on. You'll love it." Apparently I didn't have much choice in the matter, and I didn't want to make a scene. As we scooped, he drove so quickly I had to cling for dear life onto the seat of his car.

"I'm getting kind of dizzy. Can we go home?" I asked, after our third time around the loop.

"Don't you want to go to the party? Come on—we'll just go for a minute. You'll have a great time, I promise. I bet Mackenzie'll be there."

"Really? We played phone tag today and kept missing each other."

"I'm sure she'll be there."

I wanted to see Mackenzie. I couldn't wait to tell her about General Teeso. Would I ever have a normal date in my life?

He drove us several miles into the farmland surrounding Venice. We turned onto a rural road, with cars and trucks parked along the sides. Music blared nearby; smoke rose from a bonfire in the distance. Pete drove past the parked cars to a more secluded spot. "I'm looking for a good place to park," he said.

"Why don't we just park back there with the other cars?"

He braked, and then shut off the ignition. "I thought we'd park here, Sophie," he said with a glint in his eyes.

I had an inkling of what was coming. "Um, I'm gonna walk to the party," I said. I turned to open the door, but he clutched my elbow.

"Sophie," he said again. His face slackened, his eyes

closed, his lips grew thick; he morphed into a crazed muppet with a pink mouth open so wide I could practically see his tonsils. He lunged at me like a hungry amphibian.

I punched him before I knew what I was doing. I'd never punched anyone before in my life. I didn't know where it had come from—my hidden inner Mike Tyson? My fist landed in the middle of his chest.

"Ow!" He jumped back and gaped at me. "You hit me! I can't believe you just hit me! Why did you do that?"

"You lunged at me like the *Jaws* shark," I said indignantly. I hadn't meant to punch him; I'd just intended to get him to back off. I was surprised it had hurt him a little, because I didn't exactly have the biggest muscles around. And that was an understatement.

He coughed. "You knocked the wind out of me."

"Sorry."

"I can't believe I got punched by a girl." He leaned back in his seat and rubbed his forehead. "Look, you promise you won't tell anyone about this? I mean, I don't want . . . " He coughed again. "Word to get around," he said softly.

I nodded. "Okay. I promise." He wasn't a bad guy, just . . . misguided was probably the word.

He shook his head, started the car again, and reparked it where the rest of the cars were. We walked in silence to the party. In the clearing was a bonfire surrounded by three kegs and a huge crowd of football players, who instantly swallowed Pete up into their midst, leaving me all by myself.

144

I should've stayed home and eaten pizza with Colin. I walked around—being alone at a party was embarrassing. I hoped I could find someone I knew who would give me a ride home. In the orange light of the fire, people were shadowed between the grass and the corn. A stereo blared out the back of a truck. Crushed beer cans and red plastic cups lay everywhere, scattered around the clearing.

I didn't see Mackenzie or her brother. I looked through the crowd, searching for a familiar face. I walked around the perimeter, staring at the strangers in the flickering light, and then, out of the corner of my eye, I saw a tall guy with dark hair standing by himself, on the edge of the crowd. I squinted at him. Was that—?

"Colin?" I asked.

He looked up.

"What are you doing here?" I walked over to him.

"No one said it was invite only," he said. "How's the date going? Where'd you eat?"

I shook my head and stared down at the grass. "You're right. I really can pick 'em." I felt so grateful to see him my body felt limp. I opened my mouth to say something but couldn't think what.

"You okay?" he asked.

I nodded. It was nice to hear someone ask that with sincere concern. He squeezed my shoulder; he knew I wasn't exactly okay. He drew me to him and gave me a hug.

"You need a ride home?" he asked.

"Please," I said.

*　　*　　*

When I got home, Sam was already back from her date with Josh. She sat at the kitchen table, drinking a Yoo-Hoo.

"How did it go?" I asked her.

"Good news or bad news?"

"Good news," I said.

"I got us an invitation to Yom Kippur. You know how I did it? Well—here comes the bad news. Or maybe it's not so much bad, as just weird. Tonight Josh told me he really likes me, only sometimes he's bothered by the fact that I'm not Jewish, because he always pictured himself with a Jewish girl. Pretty ironic, huh?"

I took off my shoes and stretched my feet. "It's like a twisted modern-day *Yentl*."

"*Yentl in Venice*," she said. "Not a bad idea. We could make millions on Broadway. So I told him I'd like to go to Yom Kippur services with him to learn more about his culture and religion. Can you believe I said that?"

"Your acting skills are improving all the time."

"He was really excited. He said, 'I'm touched that you would do that for me.' I had a glass of wine by then and I was getting so confused by all this Jewish/not Jewish and cousin/not cousin mumbo jumbo going through my head that I said I wasn't feeling well and had to go home."

At least I wasn't the only one having major identity trouble. Sam always seemed so much more at ease with pretending we were different people—but maybe that was only on the surface. Deep inside she was clearly just as conflicted as I was about it.

"So it's okay for me to come to Yom Kippur, too?" I asked.

"I told him you were really depressed because you and Colin were having problems, and I thought it would cheer you up."

"Yom Kippur?" I asked. "It's a pretty somber holiday."

"That's exactly what he said. But I told him you just needed to be around other people right now." She chugged the rest of her Yoo-Hoo. "How was your night?"

I told her about the whole date with Pete, including the Conundrum.

"Yum," she said. "He might be onto something."

"Don't tell anyone. He'll sue me."

I didn't tell her about Colin. It had been so great to see him there, such a perfect surprise, I somehow didn't want to ruin it by talking about it, even with my sister.

10

Monday was Yom Kippur. Sam called in sick to work and picked me up at school after third period. I feigned illness to my teachers, which wasn't hard to do since I felt sick from not eating—Sam and I'd both decided to try to fast for the holiday, although we were doing it on the sly. I'd stashed a soda and a Snickers bar in the car, in case I couldn't last until dinner.

We met Josh and Leo at the Mount Sinai Synagogue in Indianapolis. It was one of the largest synagogues in the state, and the members of the Wilshire College Hillel attended services there. Afterward we planned to go to the Hillel to break the fast. We hugged Josh and Leo quickly and filed into the temple to join the service.

The air in the synagogue was chilly, but it was packed with people; there must have been three hundred or more. I couldn't believe there were this many Jews in Indiana. How had they all ended up here? Did they take a wrong turn from Brooklyn?

Throughout the services I thought about going to synagogue with my parents when I was younger. I'd listen to the rabbi chant rhythmically and sometimes I'd fall asleep on my mom's shoulder. Occasionally my dad would fall asleep, too, and start snoring; Sam and I would have to poke him to get him to stop.

After the service was over, Sam excused herself to go to the bathroom; she walked to the back of the synagogue, and stopped to scribble *Solomon* on a list of names to be read aloud at the Yizkor service, later that afternoon. We wouldn't be around to hear it read, but knowing that it would happen was enough.

As we walked out of the temple, I saw a familiar man making his way toward the rabbi in front. It took me a second to place him—the black hat and gray blazer. My chest tightened and I grabbed Sam's arm. "He's here," I whispered in her ear. "Hertznick's *here.*"

We said good-bye to Leo and Josh, trying to act natural, and scurried outside as quickly as we could. Then we ran. We bounded down the sidewalk and hopped in our car. Sam turned on the ignition. Nothing happened. She tried again. Nothing.

"*No,*" Sam said. "*Not now.*"

"Wait a minute," I said. "Pop the hood."

"Are you kidding me?"

"Just pop the hood."

I jumped outside and looked under the hood. The battery terminals were corroded. In class the other day Chester had told us to use a paste of baking soda and water to clean the battery terminals on the Chevy, but he said that in a pinch you could use Coke or Pepsi— the phosphoric acid was a heavy-duty cleaner. I

149

disconnected the terminals, got my can of Coke out of the car, and poured the whole thing on the battery. The corrosion bubbled away.

The car started on the next try. We tore out of the parking lot, with no sign of Hertznick behind us. I looked out the back window. "Why was he there? Did he see us?" My voice squeaked.

"I don't think he did." She checked the rearview mirror.

We were both breathing so hard we could barely speak. I called Difriggio on our cell phone and left him a message that we'd just seen Hertznick, but we didn't think he'd seen us. I knew Difriggio would let us have it for even stepping foot in a synagogue, but I hoped he'd understand why we'd gone. And Hertznick hadn't seen us. Hopefully. I prayed that we were safe.

After we'd driven for a while and calmed down slightly, Sam said, "I can't believe we got out of there. And I can't believe you fixed our car with Coke."

"I can't believe I did either."

She touched my arm. "So I guess you're not just staring at the guys in class."

"Not anymore." We laughed a little, nervously. Sam clutched the steering wheel so tightly her knuckles were pink. I kept looking out the back window, making sure no one was following us.

We decided to skip the break-the-fast meal at the Hillel and go right home; we could explain to Josh and Leo later that our car had broken down on the way.

Our cell phone rang a few minutes after we got home. Sam and I looked at each other. Neither of us wanted to answer it and face Difriggio's wrath. "You're older," I told her.

"You're younger, he'll be nicer to you," she said.

"You're . . ."

She took a deep breath. "I'll just get it. Here goes. Hello?" she said tentatively.

He yelled so loud I could hear him two feet away.

"Awl the HARD WORK I put into your new lives, and then this? Why? Why do you do this to me? Felix told me you're not religious. If he told me you were religious, I woulda warned you. OF COURSE HERTZNICK'S GONNA LOOK FOR YOUSE TWO IN THAT SYNAGOGUE. Biggest one in the state, on the biggest holiday? OF COURSE!" He sputtered a string of Italian.

"We—we—um—we don't think he saw us," Sam said. "We're pretty sure."

More Italian. Finally, after a few moments, Difriggio began to calm down. "All right. All right. We're going to assume he didn't see you. Next time you want to do something like that, you check with me first, okay?"

"Okay," Sam said.

"In the meantime I'm going to try to keep better tabs on Hertznick. Make sure he's steering clear of you. And you let me know whenever you leave Venice, too. Make things easier."

"Okay," Sam said. She hung up the phone.

"He was kinda mad," she said to me.

"I heard," I said.

"Oh God. What have we done?" She put her head in her hands.

151

I slept in Sam's bed that night. In my dreams Enid and Hertznick searched for us in Venice, and Sam and I hid out in the Petal Diner, crouching under the tables. Thankfully, when I woke up in the morning, I was still in Sam's bed, with her arm around me.

The next day after school, Sam, Gus, and I met at his office. Sam had done a great job cleaning the place up—she must have recycled about two tons of paper, and you could actually see the floor again. The typewriter that Gus used to peck on with two fingers had been relegated to the top of the file cabinet, replaced by the iMac Sam had ordered. She'd exchanged his ripped-up, green velour sofa for several chairs from Colin's shop. Next to the iMac sat the call-tracing apparatus; Sam and Gus had installed it together.

"The background check on Elsie Schenker came through," Gus told us. "Turns out Elsie worked in the hall of records in Chicago at the time Ruth Brauner disappeared."

"Then you think Elsie was responsible for Ruth's records disappearing?" I asked.

"I'm sure she had something to do with it," Gus said. "I'm not sure exactly how or why, but I'm willing to bet she was involved. And if so—"

The phone rang, interrupting him. I stared at it and Gus said, "Wait a second." He flipped the switch on the tracing equipment. It rang three times and then he picked up.

"This is ValueMan Vacations!" a recorded voice exclaimed. "We're happy to inform you that you are the lucky winner of—"

"Good Lord." Gus rolled his eyes and disconnected the line.

We waited for two more hours that day, hoping the mysterious caller would try again, but he didn't. I helped out at the office the next couple afternoons after school, and finally, on Thursday, another call came. Gus picked up the phone after two rings and turned on the tracing equipment.

"Jenkins Agency."

"Stop your search or you won't live to find her," the voice growled.

"All right, DeCarlo. Enjoy that painting while you've got it because you're not going to keep it for long," Gus said, speaking slowly—we had to keep him on the line for ten seconds for the trace to work.

The caller hung up.

"Did you get a trace?" Gus asked.

Sam stared at the equipment and smiled. "Got it," she said. She ran the number through a program on the computer and came up with an address. "It's a public phone on Washington Street in Chicago."

"Why would DeCarlo or one of his men call us from Chicago?" I asked.

"Maybe it's someone else," Sam said.

"Whoever it is, I think we're going to be taking a trip back to Chicago real soon," Gus said.

I hugged my elbows. "I'm coming, too. I don't want to be left behind this time." I couldn't stand the idea of being home alone while this creepy phone caller and Hal Hertznick were on the loose.

"I think it's a good idea for Sophie to come," Sam

said. I got the feeling she didn't want to leave me home alone either. "We'll all go. You need both of us."

He nodded. "All right."

Sam and Gus picked me up after school on Friday. We'd called Difriggio before we left to let him know we were going out of town.

We didn't get to Chicago until 9 P.M., so all I could see were the glittery lights of the tall buildings. Even though I'd never been there, a part of me felt like I was coming home to the big city. It seemed magical and familiar: all the people on the streets late at night, going in and out of restaurants and shops, talking and laughing. We arrived at Gus's sister's high-rise, and the doorman took our luggage into the elevator for us.

Gus's sister Rita greeted us at the door in a navy business suit. She looked just the way Sam had described her—slim and polished and nothing like Gus. She was pretty, with short, dark curly hair and brown eyes. Gus had almost no hair and blue eyes. Families were so strange.

"Sorry we're late," Gus said.

"Nice to see you again," Rita told Sam, and hugged her closely.

Rita placed her arms on my shoulders. "And this must be Sophie." She looked down at my boots. "Great shoes."

I liked her already.

"I see this girl's fashion sense hasn't rubbed off on you yet," she said to her brother.

"Hmmph," he said.

"Look at you two!" Rita said. "Never seen my brother in the company of two such fine young women before! Ever since his wife, Victoria—"

"Enough," Gus snapped, in the sharpest tone I'd ever heard him use.

"Sorry. It's just . . . you're looking good, Gus. Better than you've looked in years. Tea, anyone?" Rita offered. Sam and I nodded; she brought us steaming cups of chamomile, and a mug of coffee for Gus. I looked around her modern, sparsely furnished apartment. Everything was neat and streamlined. Hardly any photos or tchotchkes. There was one photo of Rita and Gus together as kids. I could barely recognize Gus, with a full head of hair and a plump little face. A black-and-white picture of a couple hung on the wall.

"Are those your parents?" I asked.

"Were," Rita said. "Sue and Bob Jenkins. Salt of the earth."

"What did your father do?" When I looked closely, I could see the resemblance between Gus and his dad.

"He was a cop. And his father before him, and his father before that," Rita said.

"I didn't know Gus was a legacy," Sam said.

"Law enforcement is in the Jenkins blood," Gus called out from the kitchen, where he was peering into the fridge. "Or at least it was until . . . "

"What?" I asked.

"Nothing. I think the baseball game's on."

Rita shook her head; I got the feeling Gus was holding something back. I wanted to hear more about his past—a subject we never heard him talk about, ever. He

155

was always as evasive about his previous life as we were about ours. Maybe that was why we got along so well. We seemed to have a mutual understanding that he wouldn't pick around in our backgrounds too much, and we wouldn't nose into his.

We were all tired from traveling and could barely keep our eyes open. Rita showed me the guest room—it had a huge bed with a puffy white down comforter and a view of Lake Michigan. It was so neat and pristinely clean, it felt like a hotel. Sam and I fell asleep almost as soon as our heads hit the pillows.

The next morning the four of us ate bagels at a deli around the corner. "I'm in heaven," I said. It was a real bagel, soft and doughy inside, not like the frozen Lender's ones we were forced to eat in Venice. We sat by the window and watched the crowds go by. I was thrilled to see all the different kinds of people and inhale the smells of food sold on the street and listen to the elevated subway train rumbling overhead. I loved being anonymous again, like I was back in New York. I felt safe being with Gus and Rita; I was sure that Enid's PI wouldn't find us here.

The wall of the bagel shop was plastered with posters for music, plays, and events all over the city.

"Can we go out tonight?" I asked. I leafed through the paper and saw an ad for a band I'd heard in New York, the Swells, playing at a club called Velvet. "I'd love to go hear someone really sing." With all the investigating, I'd hardly been playing my guitar and singing much at all, unless you counted the corny melodies Mrs.

156

Oderkirk led us in during music class, which I didn't. I missed singing, and I hoped that hearing some good music would inspire me to get started again.

Gus had a huge wad of cream cheese on his lip. "Go out?"

"People do that in a city," Rita told him. She turned to Sam and me. "Velvet's really close to my place. You'll love it there. It's got black velvet booths—"

"We're on a business trip, not a holiday," Gus interrupted.

I rolled my eyes.

He checked his watch. "Speaking of which, it's time to get to work. Let's go to Washington Street."

"I don't see how you're going to figure out who made the call just from taking a look at the pay phone," Rita said. "I mean, the caller could've come from anywhere in the city to use that phone."

"Don't underestimate us, Rita," Gus said.

"Sherlock Holmes could figure out exactly where a person lived just from looking at his shoes," I said.

"So if I'm wearing Jimmy Choos you can tell I'm from Chicago?"

Gus glared at her. I laughed. I liked Rita.

We drove down Washington Street until we found the right spot. It was on a downtown block surrounded by office towers, banks, and commercial buildings. A huge row of pay phones lined one corner, beside an office building. We parked right across the street, then looked at the number on each phone until we found the one where the call was made from.

"All right, sleuths. What do we do now, wait here and

see if this guy comes back?" Rita asked.

Sam shook her head. "We know the exact time and date that the call was made. A lot of these office buildings are high security these days, right? I've read that they usually videotape who comes in and out the door. There should be a shot of the phones from one of these buildings. We've just got to get the tapes."

"That's where I come in," Gus said. He took out the Chicago PD badge he kept around for such occasions, when a little extra pressure might be required. He wasn't supposed to have his badge anymore, but Gus didn't always do things by the book, exactly.

Sam and I waited in the car, since Gus thought having two young women with him might undermine his credibility as a supposed plainclothes cop. Through the window we watched Gus talk to the man at the security desk. Gus flashed his badge, and a few minutes later the man handed over the tape.

"Was that legal?" Sam asked Gus when he returned to the car.

"As Rita will tell you, *legal* can be a widely interpreted term," he said.

He went into four other buildings near the bank of pay phones and across the street, until we had tapes from all of them.

"We've got twenty-four hours to review them," Gus said.

Rita moaned. "I'm getting the feeling that after a day spent wallowing through security tapes we're not going to get to take these girls out on the town."

"It shouldn't take too long," Gus told Rita. "So long as

158

there's a clear shot of something. Here's hoping."

We drove back to Rita's apartment and rewound the first tape until we found the time that our call was received. You could make out the bank of pay phones, but the view was from across the street. We saw the two blurry legs of the man making the call, but he was unidentifiable.

From the shot of another building you couldn't see anything, and on the third one you could see one of the pay phones, and people getting in and out of taxis and cars. A man in a plaid suit got out of an old Buick, sort of like the one Sam and I had.

"He's got a suit just like yours," I told Gus. "Where do you get those hideous things?"

"Hey, I like that suit," Gus grumped.

The fourth tape had a good shot of the man making the call.

"There he is," Sam said. The film was blurry, but you could tell the man was tall and very thin and crouched over the phone awkwardly.

"Doesn't look like DeCarlo," Sam said.

"Doesn't look like anyone," Rita said. "He's a blurry mess."

But despite the blur there was something that was sort of distinctive. I squinted at the tall thin form. "That's a plaid suit," I said.

"Wait a second." Gus paused it. "She's right."

We put the third tape back in. When the plaid-suited man stepped into the car, Gus paused it.

Rita squinted at the screen. "Well, look at that."

As the man got into his car, if you looked very

closely, you could just make out the license-plate number.

Gus called one of his friends in the police department, Mark Joyner, and asked him to trace the plate for us, to find out the man's name and address. Mark said he'd do it, but he couldn't get the results back to us until the next morning.

In the meantime, we decided to pay a visit to someone else on our list—Elsie Goldfarb, née Schenker.

Elsie lived in an old apartment building in Evanston surrounded by hedges and grass, with lots of elderly people wandering about with their walkers and canes. The inside smelled like a combination of laundry and cats.

"When we were here last time we knocked on a few neighbors' doors, but no one would talk to us," Sam told me. "It seems like these people have lived in this building forever. I hope she's home now." We entered the front door behind a man in a wheelchair. "I think Sophie should be the one to knock on her door first," Sam said.

"Why me?" I asked.

"You look the youngest and friendliest. She'd be more likely to open the door to you than to Gus or me."

"You think I'm not young and friendly looking?" Gus asked.

"Is that a rhetorical question?" Sam said.

After a bumpy ride in an old clanking elevator, we reached Elsie's third-floor apartment.

I knocked. An old woman in a blue wool cardigan

opened the door, but left the chain still hooked.

"Um, hi!" I said, with the largest, cheeriest smile I could muster.

Her hair was swept into a tight white bun on top of her head. "I already bought your Girl Scout cookies," she said abruptly, and slammed the door.

I looked toward Sam and Gus and shrugged. I knocked again.

"Um . . . Mrs. Goldfarb? I've got a question for you."

She opened the door a little wider this time. "Who are you? What do you want?" Out of the corner of her eye she spied Gus and Sam in the hall, too. "What is this about?"

"We were hoping that you could help us," I said. "We know that you once worked at the hall of records, fifty years ago."

"Yes, this is true," she said tentatively. She drew her cardigan more tightly around her shoulders.

"We're trying to find an old friend of yours." I paused. "We want to reunite her with a painting—"

"I don't know anything about it," Elsie interrupted. Her eyes grew wide and her hands trembled—she was clearly lying.

"Did you know a woman named Ruth Brauner?" I asked.

She didn't answer.

Gus came closer. "It's a federal crime to destroy official documents," he said roughly. He seemed to decide the softer approach wasn't getting us far enough.

"I don't know anything!" Elsie shouted. "Please, leave me alone." She moved to close the door again. I felt a

161

twinge of guilt for upsetting her. She was an elderly, fragile woman; we couldn't push her too much.

"I'd hate to have to take this strange matter of Ruth Brauner's documents simply disappearing to the police," Gus said.

"Please—we don't want to do anything to Ruth. We want to help her," I said.

Elsie blinked at us. "That painting caused Ruth Brauner all the trouble in the world. She's not going to want it back. It's good that it's in other hands now. That painting is a curse."

"What?" I asked her.

Elsie paused, her expression pained. "I can't talk anymore. Please. Let me be." She shut the door on us.

We stood in the hall, looking at one another. Gus moved to knock on the door again but stopped himself. He shook his head. "I don't think she's going to tell us anything more."

Sam stared down the hallway. "She can't admit she did anything without risking going to jail herself."

"At least she seems to know that Ruth is alive," I said. "But why would she think Ruth wouldn't want the painting back?"

11

Gus decided it was okay for us to take the night off. Rita, Sam, and I got dressed up to go to the club.

"Tonight you'll be escorting three beautiful women, you lucky dog," Rita called out to Gus.

He was firmly planted in front of the TV, watching a football game. "Whuh?" he asked. "Rita, you have any Cheez Whiz?"

Rita sighed. "Forget it."

We finally convinced Gus to leave the TV and come out with us. I was dying for a night on the town that didn't involve a Chinese restaurant in a converted Pizza Hut, scooping the loop, or a keg party in a cornfield. Not having to punch my evening companions sounded nice, too.

I got into the club even though I was underage; the man at the door must have assumed Rita and Gus were my parents. Sam and I ordered Cokes, and Rita and Gus had beers. Soon after we were seated the show began. I closed my eyes and leaned back in our booth, soaking it in. After we finished our drinks, Rita, Sam, and I got up to dance; we even dragged Gus out to join us for a few seconds of one song. He nodded in place on the dance floor like a bobbing dashboard ornament, then quickly sat back down.

We stayed out till midnight. "That wasn't so bad, was it?" Rita asked Gus as we walked back to her apartment. He didn't answer.

"You looked great on the dance floor—good practice for the Sadie Hawkins," I told him.

"Sadie Hawkins?" Rita asked. "I wonder who will ask my brother."

"No one. I'm not going to that malarkey," Gus said.

"Not going? Right now hearts all over Venice are being broken with those words," I said.

Gus looked up at the buildings towering upward. "Why me?" he asked.

Sam and I didn't wake up until after nine the next morning. Rita was drinking coffee and reading a newspaper, and Gus was dressed and ready to go. I'd never seen him looking so lively before noon.

"I got a fax ten minutes ago," he told us. "The license plate was traced to an Arnold Berkowitz in Winnetka. I've got an address—I'm going to go."

"Okay," Sam said. "Just give us five minutes."

Gus shook his head. "I think I'm going to handle this one by myself. We don't know anything about this guy— he could be dangerous."

"How dangerous could an Arnold Berkowitz be?" Rita asked. "He sounds like a science nerd. What's he going to do, pelt you with pocket protectors?"

I laughed, but Gus glared at his sister. "I don't want to bring the girls into any potential trouble."

"I've worked on this case as much as you, Gus," Sam said. "I'm coming."

"Me, too," I said. "We got Elsie to talk yesterday."

"How about this? I'll stay with the girls in the car, and you can go in first and check out the situation. If it seems safe, we'll be right behind you," Rita said.

Gus looked uneasy.

"We'll vote on it, then," Sam said.

"All right, all right," Gus conceded. "I don't know why I pretend to have any power at all."

Winnetka looked like a pleasant suburb, not the kind of place where a threatening caller would live. We found the address—47 Cranberry Lane—a large, white, sprawling house with black shutters.

A short, plump woman in a purple nightgown with a big cloud of curly black hair answered the door. She snapped her gum. She looked safe enough, and Sam and I got out of the car and joined Gus at the front door. Gus asked if Arnold Berkowitz was home.

"Arnie? He doesn't live here anymore," she said. "What did he do now? Does he owe you money?"

"No—we just wanted to speak with him," Gus said. "Are you—a relative?"

"I'm his ex. He lives with Ruth, his mom, now," she said. "One-oh-five Poplar Street. And when you find him, tell him he's late with his check this month."

"Is that Ruth Brauner?" I asked her.

"Ruth Berkowitz," she said. "You know her?"

165

"Maybe," I said.

She wished us luck and shut the door.

"Do you think Arnold Berkowitz is Ruth Brauner's son?" I asked as we walked back to the car. My heart raced. Were we on the verge of finally finding her? I hadn't realized how much I'd wanted to meet Ruth—how much hope I'd pinned on her reunion with Leo—until it seemed almost a reality. If we could reunite Leo with Ruth after all these years, then it seemed like anything was possible.

We checked a map and sped to 105 Poplar Street. It was a stone house covered in ivy, surrounded by an overgrown garden. Wildflowers grew several feet high. We parked along the street. Sam and I stared at Gus as he got ready to approach the house. "Be careful," Sam said. Gus walked up to the front door and knocked.

A middle-aged man in a short terrycloth bathrobe answered the door. He was tall with pale, skinny legs and sheepskin slippers. It was a warm day, but he seemed to shiver.

We watched Gus nod, and the two men exchanged a few words.

Then the man suddenly slammed the door. Through the windows, we could see his terrycloth-covered figure bounding upward as he climbed the stairs.

"It's Berkowitz, all right," Gus said, coming back to the car.

"Good job," Rita said. "You scared that guy half to death."

"What happened?" I asked.

Gus sat back in the front seat of the car. He sighed. "I

just asked him his name. He flipped."

"Now what?" Rita asked.

"He's not going to be afraid of us," I said. "Why don't Sam and I try talking to him?"

Gus shook his head. "I don't know."

"He doesn't seem like much of a threat," Rita offered.

We talked it over and finally decided that Sam and I would wait for fifteen minutes and then try the front door again; Gus would join us after we got Arnold Berkowitz calmed down. We rang the bell a few times, and when Arnold didn't appear, we went around to the back. Behind the house, two sliding-glass doors opened to a large patio dotted with wrought-iron furniture.

We knocked on the glass. Nothing.

We knocked again.

Finally, he appeared at the door. He opened it a little, staying behind the screen. "What?" he said. His voice sounded near tears. "What do you want?"

"We're looking for Ruth Brauner," Sam said.

He stood frozen, staring at us.

"We work for Leo Shattenberg—we discovered a painting—" I began.

He turned white. "I'm going upstairs now, and you need to go away."

Gus appeared behind us then; Arnold went even paler. "We know you made those phone calls, Berkowitz," Gus said. "If you don't answer a few questions for us, we're going to press charges. We need you to tell us about Ruth Brauner, and an Ivan Sebrid painting."

"We don't want the painting. We don't want

anything to do with it," Arnold said.

"That's what Elsie said," I told him. "Why?"

"Look, don't you see?" His voice was nearly a whisper. "If we make a claim for that painting, my mom and I are going to be killed."

"What?" Sam asked. "By who?"

He wouldn't answer.

"Is Ruth Brauner your mother?" I asked.

A small, elderly woman appeared behind him in the doorway. She wore a yellow dress and her white hair was pinned up loosely.

"Yes, I am," she said.

"Ruth Brauner?" I asked. "You're Ruth Brauner?" I thought my heart was going to drop onto the patio.

"Mom, go back upstairs," Arnold told his mother. "I'll handle this. The name's Berkowitz. My mom married my dad, Harold Berkowitz."

"Arnie, what's going on out here?" Ruth asked.

"Nothing, Mom. Go back upstairs."

"We've been hired by Leo Shattenberg to find you," I told her.

"Leo?" she asked in a barely audible whisper. She held the door frame, steadying herself.

"Now you need to leave us alone," Arnold said, attempting to be brazen. "Or I'm going to call the police!"

Ruth laid a hand on his shoulder. "Arnie—please. I want to talk to these people."

Ruth Brauner—or Ruth Berkowitz, as she was known now—invited Sam, Gus, and me to talk out on the

168

patio. We got Rita from the car and she joined us, too. Ruth sat down slowly into a chair with a striped blue cushion. She asked Arnie to bring us some tea.

"Mom—why? Why do you want to do this?" Arnold whined.

"This is my house, Arnie. I'll do what I like. Bring out some of that chocolate cake, too, please."

Through the window, we watched Arnie put a kettle on the stove and place a chocolate cake on the kitchen table.

"My son and his wife are getting a divorce," Ruth said. "He's living here while the divorce is being settled. My husband Harold passed away twenty years ago."

She was so tiny and had such a soft, soothing voice; I couldn't believe that we'd finally found her. What would Leo say?

"Tell me about Leo Shattenberg," Ruth said. Her voice grew quieter when she said his name. She stared at the garden. We filled her in about Leo, and everything we'd learned about the Sebrid painting and how she was entitled to have it back.

Arnold brought out cups and spoons. "This is all my fault, Mom," he said. "After Elsie heard a PI had been talking to her neighbors a few weeks ago, she was scared. She called me—she was really upset. I called the numbers on the card these people left under her door, and told them to stay away. That's all I did." He turned to us. He seemed calmer now and less frightened, now that his mother was beside him. He relaxed a little as he told the story.

"Why didn't you want us to find you?" I asked him.

"My mom never wanted anything to do with her past. She told me once in passing that her family had owned an Ivan Sebrid painting, but she didn't like to talk about what happened to it. She never really talked about her childhood or her family—all I knew was she'd escaped Europe, but the rest of her family didn't." He touched his mother's shoulder. "Are you okay, Mom? Are you okay that I'm telling them all this?"

"It's all right," she said. "I'm all right."

"Then a few months ago, while I was moving in here, I found a box hidden in the closet. Inside were some old, weathered photos. One picture was of my mom as a child in Vienna with her family—and in the background of the picture was the painting *Lovers in the Village*. I'd read that the painting had been put on display at the Aldredge Museum. I did some research, and I found out that DeCarlo owned it. I went to see him and told him I was looking into the painting's provenance. He threatened me—he said if I made a claim, my mother and I would be in trouble. I decided I didn't want anything to do with it after that. I didn't tell my mother about it—I didn't want her to know and be afraid. That's why I tried to get you off the case."

"DeCarlo?" Ruth clenched her hands. "Roderick DeCarlo?"

"Roderick?" Arnold asked. "No, Mom—who's Roderick?"

"Roderick DeCarlo was Dale's father. He died six months ago," Gus said. "Did you know him?" he asked Ruth.

She pressed her lips together. "I met that man when I

170

was twenty-three years old. I had contacted him because I heard that he might have a clue to the whereabouts of my family's painting. I didn't know when I tried to contact him that he had the painting himself."

"How did he get it?" I asked.

She hesitated and frowned slightly. "When the war started, my parents smuggled me out of Vienna on a truck bound for London. My parents stored the painting in a vault; they told me where it was and how I could come back and get it, if anything happened. I never saw my parents again." She paused and gazed at the ground. "When the war ended, I made a few inquiries into how I might go about opening the vault and retrieving the painting from overseas. I was told to contact Roderick DeCarlo, and I did. I wrote to him, asking where my painting was. I heard nothing back for many months— until he showed up at my boardinghouse in Chicago. He said the painting was no longer mine, and he was watching me." Her voice wavered. "He said if I wasn't careful, Leo and I would never be heard from again."

Sam asked, "Is that why you ran away?"

She nodded solemnly.

"And Elsie wiped out your identity," Gus said.

"I paid her to do it. It was the only way I could think to save Leo. I was young and had lost my whole family—I couldn't bear the thought of losing anyone else. DeCarlo was clearly capable of hurting Leo or me, or hiring someone who would. Elsie was the only one who knew the reason why I left. I never told Leo, or anybody else. I knew if I told Leo he would confront DeCarlo. I decided I'd rather not be with him than put

171

his life in danger. Enough people who I'd loved had died. I couldn't let anything happen to Leo."

Arnold stared at Gus. "Am I going to be arrested for making those calls? You said it would be okay if I talked to you—that you wouldn't press charges, right?"

"We're not pressing charges," Gus said. "But we're going to report back to our client. I'd like to call him now, and let him know we've located you."

"You're going to call Leo Shattenberg now?" Ruth asked. There was a note of hope in her voice.

"If that's all right with you," Gus said.

Ruth nodded. Gus stepped out into the backyard and called Leo on his cell phone—he waved Sam and me over, and we spoke with Leo, too, and told him everything Ruth had said to us. Leo wanted to come see Ruth as soon as possible.

"It's been so many years," he said on the phone. "I'd like to see her tonight, or tomorrow, if she will."

Ruth agreed to see Leo that night. Sam, Gus, and I returned to Rita's apartment for dinner, and later we drove back to Ruth's. Leo and Josh arrived soon after, and when Leo saw Ruth again for the first time, there was an awkward moment as they stood looking at each other. They smiled and seemed bewildered by all the time that had passed.

"You look exactly the same," Leo told her.

"You do, too," Ruth said.

While Leo and Ruth took a long walk around the neighborhood, Gus talked to Arnold in the living room about pressing charges against Dale DeCarlo. Sam, Josh, and I sat on the patio.

"So you really found her," Josh said. "I can't believe it. I always thought he had a good life with my grandmother, but I've never seen him like this. I guess what he and Ruth had was a unique, rare thing."

When Leo and Ruth came back from their walk, Ruth said she needed to lie down for a while; all the excitement of the day had exhausted her. Arnold took her upstairs, and Leo and Gus joined us on the patio.

Leo sat in a wrought-iron chair. As the sun began to set, the patio lights came on, casting a yellow glow over the garden. He told us everything Ruth had said.

"Roderick DeCarlo was the man Ruth was seen with at the boardinghouse, the day she left me. He must have passed the painting on to his son when he died, and Dale DeCarlo decided to show it at the museum—a foolhardy decision—he'd probably hoped that the museum show would push the price up so that he could sell it for even more money."

Leo stared down at the tiles on the patio and fiddled with his hands in his lap.

"She did tell me she tried to look for me once—after her husband died, she'd begun to have regrets about what she'd done. She hired someone to find me. And do you know what the man found? He couldn't locate me, but he managed to track down a Leo Shattenberg who was also from Poland originally and had descendants in New York City. But that Leo had died in the war and wasn't related to me."

"Another Leo Shattenberg?" Sam's voice cracked.

"A totally different one," Leo said. "No relation whatsoever. Can you believe that? Ruth took it as a sign that

173

she should stop looking for me, that it was a dead end. She gave up after that."

"Where in New York City did the relatives of the other Leo Shattenberg live?" I asked, my voice hollow.

"Queens, I believe," he said. "What was the name of the neighborhood? Riverside? No. Sunnyside."

"She gave up," I echoed. I stared at the overgrown garden. "Another, unrelated Leo Shattenberg."

Gus looked at us strangely. I tried to hide my disappointment. It seemed like a cruel joke, that there should be two people with that name. That here we were again, Sam and I, alone.

Arnold returned from upstairs; I asked if I could please use his bathroom. Sam excused herself, too.

We both shut ourselves in the bathroom. I sat on the edge of the tub and put my head on my lap.

"It's not so bad, Sophie. I mean . . . even if they're not our family, we still know them. We're friends with them."

But friends didn't seem comparable to family. "You're just happy because you can go out with Josh now."

She smiled. "Well, who knows what will happen with that. I guess the thing is, family or not . . . you just don't have control over the future. I mean, look what happened to Ruth—she lost her whole family and let go of Leo, even though she loved him. I think . . . we're doing okay, right, Sopheleh?" I blinked—that was my dad's nickname for me. "We're doing okay on our own. We've got Gus, and Colin, Mackenzie, Wilda . . . "

Sam sat down next to me on the edge of the tub and put her arm around me. We stayed there for a while,

174

until I felt a little better. Finally, we went out to join everyone on the patio.

Ruth had awoken from her nap. We talked about the painting, and how it had brought Leo and Ruth back together. Ruth smoothed her dress, and then spoke. "I'd like to have my painting back."

Arnold moved beside her. "We can't." He reminded her about DeCarlo. "Mom, it's not worth the risk."

"Over fifty years have passed," she said. "It's all I have of my family now. I think it should be returned."

"I'm sure Dale DeCarlo's all bluff," Gus said. "He's not going to come after you. It's just his tactic to scare you off."

"But how do you know?" Arnold asked him.

"It would be too public in this case—Holocaust art claims get a lot of press these days. There's no way he could risk it."

"There's a problem, though," Leo said. "As Sam and Sophie found, the signature's no longer on the back. It will be difficult for Ruth to prove that it's hers."

"Well," I said, "that's not exactly certain yet." I thought about Colin's idea. I knew what we had to do.

12

I explained Colin's plan to my sister and Gus during the drive back to Venice. Gus barked from behind the steering wheel, "The matter is not open to discussion. You're not breaking into the museum to take a picture of the back of that painting."

"We really don't have another choice, though," Sam said. "If we can prove the signature is there, DeCarlo will have to give the painting back. And he won't expose us for the way we found out the painting's Ruth's, because he won't want any of this to become public knowledge."

I told them how Colin had said that he and I together would be in much less danger if we got caught than Sam or Gus would. "Not that we would get caught," I assured them. "But I think you should let us handle this one."

"If you do get caught, I'm not bailing you out. I've got to put my foot down sometime and draw the line," Gus said.

"Come on, didn't you do any risky business while

you were on the force all those years? I'm sure you did," I said.

"That's different," Gus said. "Also, if I bent the law a little, I didn't tell my superiors."

"Aha," I said. "I think that needs to be our new tactic for a healthy working relationship."

Gus hunched over the steering wheel. "Hmmph."

I was surprised that Sam was willing to let Colin and me do it. It was probably her conversation with Difriggio when we got home that night that relaxed her.

"Good news," she told me when she hung up the phone. "Difriggio said Hertznick followed our lead and hopped a flight to Mexico this morning."

I sank down in my chair. "I hope he stays there."

"Me, too," she said. "For a long, long time."

On Wednesday afternoon Colin, Sam, Mackenzie, and Fred and I got together in Colin's shop. Fred gave Colin a thorough lesson on how to set up the tripod and the camera for a long exposure. Mackenzie supplied a book on Bruce Busby's sculptures so we could see how the openings to the tents worked. We studied our map of the museum and planned our route. Sam paced nervously around Colin's shop, tapping her fingers on random pieces of furniture. She stopped in front of a shelf of toys. She picked up a boomerang.

"You can use this, like in *How to Steal a Million*. Remember?" she asked me. "Audrey Hepburn and Peter O'Toole fling it to hit the laser beams and set off the alarm in the museum. Then they run and hide in a broom closet. The police come, and they set the alarm off two more times until the neighbors who live across the street from the museum complain and get them to turn the alarm off. When the motion sensors in the gallery go off, you can call us, and Fred, Mackenzie, and I will take turns calling to complain about the alarm until it's shut off."

"You really think that's necessary?" Mackenzie asked. "Security seemed so lax when we were there last time."

"That was during the daytime. The place must be teeming with alarms at night. Don't forget this." Sam handed me a cigarette lighter and instructions she'd downloaded from the Internet, about how you could disable alarm wires with it. "Also, Sophie, you should keep the cell phone with you in case of an emergency. And if you do get caught, you're going to tell security it's only a prank, right?"

"Of course," I said.

"We'll be fine," Colin told her for the hundredth time. "We're not going to get caught. And anyway you've done much riskier things." I knew he was referring to the time Sam and I broke into Noelle McBride's house.

"Just be careful. Promise me you'll be careful," Sam said.

We promised we would.

Sweat beaded on my forehead as we approached the Aldredge Museum. Colin had suggested that we wear colored T-shirts with our black pants and carry our black turtlenecks in our knapsacks to put on later—we didn't want to look too conspicuous, since hardly anyone in

Indiana wore all black (except me). I held my breath as we walked past the security guards at the entrance. I was afraid they might search my knapsack, which was filled with supplies: headlamps, gloves, black hats, rope, duct tape, the UV light, the camera and folding tripod, a lock pick made out of bicycle spokes, boomerang, and the cigarette lighter.

Fred had even gotten us headsets to talk to each other if we got separated—he borrowed them from his aunt, a trucking-company dispatcher. I'd prepared for the occasion by watching *How to Steal a Million, The Thomas Crown Affair,* and *Mission Impossible.* I wanted to be ready for anything.

We pretended to be soaking up all the art in the museum, especially the Bruce Busby exhibit. I searched for motion detectors, LED lights, and security cameras surrounding the artwork.

"Did you see anything?" Colin whispered when we stood in the empty hall outside the Sebrid room.

I shook my head. "I don't see any cameras or alarms or anything. Maybe they're all hidden, though."

At a quarter to five, a guard lazily strolled through the halls announcing, "Museum's closing in fifteen minutes."

Colin and I walked to the Bruce Busby gallery. The room was deserted. Colin lifted the flap to a green, orange, and blue tent, adorned with geometrical designs. It looked like a spaceship. I climbed inside; he came in right after me. Then he closed the flap behind us.

My heart pounded so loudly I could feel it through

my whole body. Colin crouched beside me. I started to shake with fear, and he put an arm around me to calm me down. I felt so much better lying next to him. He smelled like soap. I felt a strange shiver of excitement being in his arms, our faces nearly touching. When footsteps paced down the hallway—*clump, clump, clump, clump*—and the beam of a flashlight bounced around the walls, I buried my face in his shirt.

The footsteps faded away. We waited in the tent for a long time until we were sure the coast was clear. Finally Colin whispered, "Let's go."

A part of me wished I could just stay in the tent, safe in his arms. But it was time to get started. We took off our sneakers and left them inside the tent so we could pad to the gallery quietly, without them squeaking on the shiny floors. I flicked on my headlamp, and we put on gloves. After peeking to make sure no one was in sight, we crept to the gallery with the Sebrid painting.

"Wait," I told Colin. "We need to set the motion sensors off."

"You think there really are motion sensors?"

I nodded. "There has to be something—that painting's worth so much." I took the boomerang out of my knapsack, held my breath, pretended I was Audrey Hepburn, and flung it into the room. It flailed through the air—although instead of gracefully winging back to me as it did in the film, it clunked against a ceiling fan, thudded into the far wall, and clattered onto the floor.

We listened to the silence. "I guess it's safe," Colin said after a moment. "Let's get started."

I picked the boomerang up off the floor, feeling

ridiculous. I shook my head. "Thankfully the Aldredge Museum isn't exactly the Metropolitan." Signs in the Aldredge advertised classes in making cornhusk dolls and learning quilting techniques. We'd been making such a racket, I was surprised the entire Indianapolis police force hadn't been alerted. "They might as well put a sign up—'Come Steal Our Paintings! Please!'"

I put my headset on. I agreed to watch the hallway and make sure the guard didn't come back while Colin set up the tripod and camera. I put the earphones on and whispered, "Testing, testing, one, two, three."

Colin gave me a thumbs-up. I took my place as sentry in the hall, shifting my weight on my feet, trying not to shake. Everything was quiet until suddenly, out of nowhere, a noise like crashing thunder blasted from the headset to my eardrums. I ran to where Colin stood.

"What was that?!" my voice squeaked.

"Sorry," he whispered. "I sneezed."

I took off my headset. "I'm just gonna stay here with you."

He fiddled with the tripod, the camera, and the UV light. We lifted the Sebrid painting off the wall, exposing its back. With the UV light beaming onto it, I could just make out what it said. The writing was fuzzy, faint, slanted, in an old German script:

An die Familie Brauner
mit freundlichen Grussen,
Ivan Sebrid 14. April 1920

*   *   *

Brauner. "It's here." I clasped Colin's hand. "Do you know any German?" I whispered.

"Just a few words . . . I think it says 'to the Brauner family . . . with pancakes'?"

"That can't be right," I said. "Are you sure?"

"No, wait, 'with affection.' Something like that," he said.

I smiled at him. This was exactly what we'd wanted.

When the exposure had finished, we hung the painting back up. We barely had it back in place when we heard something.

Footsteps. And then a man's voice. Colin clutched my shoulder.

"Someday they'll show my caves here. Yeah. Of course I get my own set of keys. I'm pretty important around here. Yeah. It is romantic. There's this room we can lie down in . . . "

A woman giggled.

I recognized the man's voice—it was the Gnome. Lights were flipping on at the other end of the hall.

"We've got to get out of here," Colin whispered. "Quick."

From the map of the museum that we'd reviewed I knew that a staircase to the offices was to the left. The hall was so dark I couldn't find the door. I shone my light everywhere, until finally it came to a handle. A sign on the door read DO NOT PUSH – ALARM WILL SOUND. We didn't have time to pull out the lighter and attempt to defuse the alarm. I pushed the door.

The alarm clanged through the building as Colin and I ran for our lives. We flew down the two flights, Colin carrying the camera and tripod, still in our socks—we'd left our shoes inside the Busby sculpture.

Colin's car was just around the corner. We jumped inside.

"I don't think he saw us," he said as he started the ignition. "I think we're okay." He careened down the street and we sped home to Venice. We hugged good night on my porch, our stomachs still whirring.

Gus came over to our house Sunday morning to read an article from the *Indiana Eagle* to us out loud.

THEFT ATTEMPT ON BUSBY SCULPTURE

Two pairs of shoes were found inside a Bruce Busby sculpture Saturday night at the Aldredge Museum in Indianapolis. Museum officials believe a theft attempt was made on Busby's well-known tent series. However, museum guard Orin Hickles followed his "sixth sense" to the museum that night and caught the thieves in the act. Unfortunately the thieves were able to escape through one of the museum's side exits. Authorities have no leads on suspects besides the shoes, which were identified as a pair of men's Adidas sneakers, size ten, and a pair of women's black Puma sneakers, size five.

"Security is always tight at the Aldredge," Hickles told the *Eagle*. "We're the best guards around."

"I wonder whose size-five shoes those could be," Gus said, folding up the paper and sitting down at our kitchen table.

183

I bit into my toast and shrugged. "Beats me."

Sam stirred her cereal. "I wonder."

"I see," Gus said. "When's the photo going to be developed?"

"Fred says he'll have it by tomorrow."

Gus shook his head.

"Hey, can I keep that copy of the paper? I want to put that article in my scrapbook," I said.

Gus rolled up the newspaper. Then he whacked me on the head with it.

EPILOGUE

Sam, Gus, and I ate dinner at the Petal on Sunday night to celebrate our successful case.

"I talked to Leo. Ruth's not going to sell the painting when she gets it back. She wants to keep it," Gus said. He shrugged. "I guess some people are sentimental."

"You would sell it?" Sam asked. "You can't even bring yourself to throw out old ham sandwiches and ancient holiday boxer shorts."

"Those aren't worth a million dollars," Gus said. "As far as I know." He bit into his burger. "Leo said she'll send it on loan for exhibits. And I finally convinced Arnold to press charges against DeCarlo for his threat. Even if DeCarlo's not convicted, buyers will certainly be wary of purchasing anything from him in the future."

Wilda came over to our table with a strawberry pie as big as a full moon. "So who are we all taking to the Sadie Hawkins Dance Friday?" she asked us.

"Oh God," I said. I'd forgotten about that.

"Sadie Hawkins," Gus grumbled. "Just what this town needs. Can't we get through a month without a parade,

185

a dance, a whatever?" He threw up his hands.

Wilda set down some dessert forks. "A Sadie Hawkins is fun, Gus. And this one's for a good cause. They've already raised three hundred dollars for the canal."

"Save the Canal." He shook his head. "As if we'll live long enough to see that happen."

Wilda cut the pie. "I think it'll be a hoot. Who are you going to ask, Sophie?"

I shrugged. "No idea."

"Sam?"

She shrugged, too.

"Why don't you ask your cat Betty," Gus told Wilda.

She glared at him. "Someone's not getting any pie tonight." She gave slices to Sam and me but not to Gus.

I turned to Wilda. "Who are you going to ask?"

"Well, I don't know," she said. "All the men in this dust bowl are taken. It's not easy being a hot number like myself here. Slim pickings." She adjusted a pink barrette in her bright orange hair.

Gus excused himself to the bathroom. When he was gone, I asked Wilda, "What about Gus? He needs to get out of the house more. Why don't you ask him?"

"You're kidding me, right?" She wiped down the counter.

"It would do him good," I said. "Think of it as . . . community service."

She refilled his coffee mug. "He does need someone to show him a good time. And I know how to do that."

"Do you know he asked me once if I thought you'd ever get married again?" Sam told her. That wasn't exactly true—he'd said, "Is Wildabeast going to marry Betty or what?" But we'd read a few things into it.

Wilda put her hand on her hip. "Did he really?"

Sam nodded.

"You think I should ask him?"

"It'll be the best time he's had in years," Sam said.

"Hmm." Wilda walked off with her coffeepot, toward another table.

"Why haven't you asked Josh?" I asked Sam when Wilda was out of earshot. "Especially since we now know you don't share any genes."

She shrugged. Do you think he'd say yes?"

"I'm sure he would. You have to ask him. You don't want to spend the next fifty years wondering if he was really your true love," I said.

Mackenzie arrived, out of breath. She plopped down next to me in our booth. "You guys talking about the Sadie Hawkins?"

We nodded. "Who are you going with?" Sam asked her.

"I asked Fred. He's already called me twice this week to see what color dress I'm wearing so the corsage he gets will match."

"That's very considerate," I said.

"I'm a little worried about what he's going to wear. He's been eyeing some blue suede outfit at Second Hand Rose." Mackenzie locked her arm in mine. "And what about you? It's getting down to the wire."

I sighed and sipped my iced tea. Betty sauntered through the diner and curled around my ankles. "I'm going with Betty."

Wilda brought Mackenzie a glass of water. "Why don't you give that quarterback another chance?" Wilda asked me.

"The Perverted Muppet? Nah. That's not going to happen."

"How about . . . Henry the cafeteria man?" Mackenzie asked.

"You're a sicko."

"Mr. Nichols?" Mackenzie asked.

"That's illegal."

"Chester?" Sam asked.

"Stop. I'll go by myself. I don't care."

"Why don't you just go with Colin?" Sam asked me.

I was about to tell her I was thinking about asking him when Mackenzie said, "I heard Patty Harper from English class asked him."

"Oh." My insides sank. In the back of my mind I'd assumed he'd be there to go with me, if I asked—I hadn't thought about the possibility of him going with somebody else.

After we'd eaten two slices of strawberry pie each, Sam and I said good night to Gus, Wilda, and Mackenzie and walked home. "I'm just going to stop by Colin's for a second," I told Sam on our way.

The lights were on inside his shop. I found him in the back, fixing a bicycle tire.

He looked up and smiled. "Hi, Soph."

"Sam and Mackenzie and I were just at the Petal . . . I think we convinced Wilda to ask Gus to the dance," I told him.

"I can't really picture Gus square-dancing, can you?"

188

He imitated a curmudgeonly Gus trying to grumpily do-si-do.

I laughed. He pushed a patched tube back into the tire. I rummaged through a box of dusty old record albums on the floor. I picked up *The Best of Blondie* and the Go-Go's *Beauty and the Beat.*

"I got an entire Eighties record stash at a yard sale this morning for fifty cents," Colin explained.

My fingertips rested on the picture of the Go-Go's in their towels and face masks. "So I heard you and Patty are going to the dance." I tried to sound casual.

"Oh. No—I told her I wasn't sure I was going to go—that I just wasn't really into the whole thing. So she asked Larry Jackson instead."

"Really?"

He wiped his hands on a rag. "Who have you asked?"

"Nobody. I haven't had time to think about it really, we've been so busy breaking into museums and everything." I turned toward the bookshelves and scanned them as I had a hundred times in his shop. "Are you sure you don't want to go?"

"Why?" He stopped what he was doing and gazed at me.

"Well—I mean, if you wanted, we could go . . . "

"Are you asking me to the dance?"

"Not if you're going to say no, I'm not."

"What if I said yes?"

"Well, you already turned down Patty. But we're friends. It's different. Right?"

"Right." He grinned. "It's different."

189

"Is that a yes, then?"

He nodded. "Yes."

At home, I sat across from Sam at the kitchen table, phone in hand. "You have to ask him. Even if it's just as friends, or noncousins, or whatever. Just see if he's busy. It's no big deal," I told her.

"What if he says no?"

"He's not going to say no."

She shook her head. "I can't do it."

"If you're not going to call him, I'm doing it for you."

She reached for the phone and chased me, but I shut myself in the bathroom, locked the door, and dialed Josh's number.

She pounded on the door. "Gimme the phone."

"Hi, Josh? It's Sophie. Listen, the students at my school are selling tickets to this, um, fund-raising Sadie Hawkins Dance? And . . . my sister wants to ask you something."

I unlocked the door and handed her the phone. She looked like she wanted to murder me. I folded my arms and listened to their conversation.

"Josh? Hi. Fine. Yeah. Um, uh, how's Wilshire? Good weather? Great. Great. Okay. Would-you-like-to-go-to-the-Sadie-Hawkins-dance-with-me?" she spat out in her quickest New Yorkese. He didn't understand her, so she had to repeat it again, slowly.

"You would? Really? Okay. Great. Okay. Bye!" She was so flustered she forgot to tell him when it was. She called him back and told him to pick her up at eight.

*   *   *

190

The dance was full of surprises—Fern and Henry, from the school office and cafeteria, arrived together. Henry kept grumbling at everyone as he bumped into them with each square-dance move. "My dog Isabel hates men, but for some reason she's got a soft spot for Henry, so he must have a good heart in there somewhere," Fern told me at the punch bowl.

Mackenzie wore a black dress so she wouldn't clash with Fred's blue suede suit. He brought her a corsage of yellow roses.

Gus and Wilda arrived together, and though he refused to square-dance, I actually saw him smile at Wilda once by the side of the gym and tap his foot to the fiddle music.

Chester, my mechanics teacher, was the square-dance caller:

Everybody home and everybody swing . . . step right back and watch her smile, step right up and swing her awhile, first time you meet her pat her on the head and the next time you meet her feed her corn bread.

Colin and I kept laughing and stepping on each other's feet.

During a break from dancing, Sam and I went to the bathroom together. We locked the door; there was no one else around. Then she told me, "Sophie, I like him so much, but . . . he keeps asking so many questions. I mean, how can I get close to him without him finding out who we really are?"

191

"Tell me about it," I said. "Just tonight Colin said to me, as we drove to the dance, 'I feel like I know you so well now, but there's still so much I don't know. You're still a mystery,' he said. I guess it's all a risk, isn't it?"

"I guess so. Do you know what Josh told me? He said Leo went over to Ruth's with little pieces of chocolate carved into different shapes, just like he did fifty years ago. Leo told him it's complicated, seeing each other again has brought up all sorts of strange feelings . . . but for both of them, that old love is still there. It's just been buried for years under all this other stuff."

We walked back into the gym, our elbows entwined. A photographer had set up shop among the hay bales. Wilda, Gus, Mackenzie, Fred, Sam, Josh, and Colin and I all sat on the pile of hay together while he took the picture.

When I got a copy of the photo a few days later, I framed it and put it on my night table. The photo stood next to my Sherlock Holmes cap, a ring that was my mom's, a necklace that had once belonged to Viv, and a snow globe of the Brooklyn Bridge, which was my father's. Every night before I went to sleep I stared at all these artifacts of the people I loved. Then I opened the red leather-bound journal Colin had given me when he got back from London, and started to write about chocolates, Conundrums, square dancing, the people I missed, and the people I'd found.

If you enjoyed this book,
join Sophie and Sam in

Case #3:
The Venetian
Policeman

Turn the page to read the first chapter.

1

"So is he a good kisser?" I asked.

Sam scowled. "That's none of your business."

"Of course it's my business. You're my sister," I said.

We were sitting in our favorite booth at the Petal Diner on a Sunday night in November, eating a three-course dinner of pink beet-and-potato soup, roasted salmon, and cherry cupcakes with pink-rose petal frosting (Wilda, the owner and chef, was trying out a new pink menu)—all for $3.99. I'm mentioning the price because being from New York City, I never stopped being astounded by the value of things in Indiana. In fact, even after four months, most things in Indiana continued to astound me. Sometimes I'd fall asleep on the bus home from school and then wake up expecting to see sprawling cement and high-rises; I always flinched at the surprise of oceans of corn and the occasional yard sign shouting, RABBITS: PETS OR MEAT.

That night the Petal Diner buzzed with activity; Sunday nights were one of the busiest of the week, probably because it was the only place open on Sunday

197

for miles around.

"Well, does he use more tongue or lips? Does he slobber?" I asked Sam.

"Slobber? He's not a puppy."

I shrugged. "Some guys slobber. Randy Chaefsky—"

She made a face. "Randy Chaefsky slobbered?"

I nodded solemnly. "It was grim. In fact—"

She shook her head. "Spare me the gory details." Sam was closer to me than anyone in the world, but we'd never talked about guys that much, probably because there hadn't been that many guys in our lives to talk about. My physical experience with the less-fair sex was limited to one brief, random makeout session with Randy on the subway coming home from my old school, LaGuardia High School of Music and the Arts in New York City. I'd had dates with two guys since we'd come to Venice, Indiana—Troy Howard and Pete Teagarden—but neither date had resulted in the kind of passion you read about in romance novels. I hadn't even kissed either of them. Troy had turned out to be a philandering Neanderthal, and Pete, despite considering himself to be worldly and sophisticated, would probably pronounce bagel as "bagelle."

"You have to give me some details on Josh," I said. "Seeing as I have no love life whatsoever, I need to live vicariously through you. Does he call you his girlfriend?"

"Girlfriend? I don't know. It's only been a few weeks since I've known for certain he wasn't our cousin," she said.

Sam had met the guy she was dating, Josh Shattenberg,

while we were attempting to solve our last missing-persons case—Josh's grandfather, Leo Shattenberg, had hired us and our boss, Gus Jenkins, to find Leo's old girlfriend. Because Shattenberg was our real last name, too, we'd thought that Leo and Josh might be our long-lost relatives. It turned out that they weren't, which was good since sparks were flying so noticeably between Josh and my sister that I couldn't keep myself from making hillbilly cousin-mating jokes.

We hadn't been able to come right out and ask Leo and Josh if they were related to us because as far as they and everyone else in Indiana knew, we were Sam Scott and Fiona (nicknamed Sophie) Scott from Cleveland. Unbeknownst to them, our real names were Samantha and Sophia Shattenberg, of Sunnyside, Queens. Our mother had died six years ago and our dad died earlier that summer, leaving our penny-pinching, morose stepmother Enid to inherit everything. Enid had wanted to separate Sam and me, and to ship me off to a god-forsaken boarding school in the Canadian wilderness. To prevent that from happening, my sister surreptitiously transferred our dad's money into an account of our own, we fled New York City, and ended up here in Venice, Indiana, which calls itself the "Europe of the Midwest" even though most of the town's inhabitants have never ventured past Muncie.

Wilda came over to our table. She wore pink eye shadow and a necklace strung with little black cats resembling her cat, Betty, who was sprawled across the diner's welcome mat.

"Still no sign of Gus?" Wilda asked.

199

Sam shook her head. "He said he'd meet us here over an hour ago." Sam worked for Gus full-time at the Jenkins Detective Agency, and I helped out after school and on weekends. Sam was seventeen, two years older than me, and should have been starting NYU this semester, but as part of our new identities, she'd become twenty-one and my legal guardian.

Sam glanced at her cell phone. "I keep trying Gus at home, but he's not there."

"Well, I guess I'll just give you these now. I've got one for Gus, too, but I'll give him his when he shows up." Wilda reached into her apron and fished out two turkey-shaped cards.

You are cordially invited to
Wilda's Twelfth Annual Turkeyluck Dinner
Thanksgiving Day
4 P.M.
The Petal Diner
Please bring a favorite dish to share

"Turkeyluck?" Sam asked.

"It's Thanksgiving, and a potluck, so years back Chester started calling it Turkeyluck, and well, the name stuck. I invite everyone in town who doesn't have a big traditional family dinner to go to—last year Gus, Fern, Ethel, Henry, Chester and his wife, and a few others came. I make the turkey and a few pies, and everybody else brings side dishes. Last year Ethel brought the most delicious corn dogs . . . Fern made some gorgeous Sea Foam Salad. I think Gus brought a cheeseball."

"We'd love to come," I said, though my voice hesitated, and it wasn't just due to the mention of a cheeseball, which, for the uninitiated, is like a miniature bowling ball of cheese rolled in nuts or bacon bits. The problem with Thanksgiving is that when you don't have a traditional family, holidays aren't the most carefree and enjoyable part of the year. It was hard not to think about our regular Shattenberg Thanksgivings, with our mom and dad. My dad always cooked a big turkey that we could never finish. Sam and I complained about the turkey à la king we'd have for the entire week afterward —we never liked it. Now I'd give anything for turkey à la king made by my dad. Why hadn't I appreciated it then? It seemed like such a luxury now to be able to complain about the food your parents make.

Wilda must have sensed my reservations because she said, "I promise it'll be a meal you won't forget. I'm going to—"

"Garçon!" a voice interrupted from across the diner, in an embarrassingly inept French accent. It was police officer Alby. He was sharing a booth with Agnes Leary, who owned the Romancing the Stone jewelry shop on Main Street.

"Just a minute," Wilda told him sharply. She looked back at us. "I'm glad you can make it. You'll—"

"GARÇON!" Alby's voice rang out, louder.

Wilda rolled her eyes. "I'll be right back," she told us.

I stared at Alby. He wasn't looking like his usual self. Alby and his brother, Chief Callowe, comprised the entire Venice police force, and Alby was generally known as the laughingstock of it. Tonight, instead of his usual blue uniform, he wore a green polyester shirt with a large gold chain dangling down his chest. He looked like a stuffed sausage in his tight black jeans. He handed the menu to Wilda. "Steak with cheese sauce, sides of bacon, sausage, baloney, three slices of American cheese, and extra mayo. No bread. No noodles. No potato. I don't even want to see any carbohydrates on the table."

"What's up with him?" I whispered to Wilda when she came back to our table.

"Atkins diet," she muttered. "No starches whatsoever." She rolled her eyes. "He's on this whole self-improvement kick. He moved out of his mom's house, got his own place, and carries around a backpack full of self-help books these days. The other morning he sat at the counter reading *Mars and Venus in the Bedroom*."

"Eww," I said. The idea of Alby in bed was not what you wanted to think about while eating.

"Another time he was reading *Creating Respect: How to Get What You Don't Think You Deserve*," Wilda said. "This diet is the worst, though. No bread! No potatoes! The other day he ordered my chicken fried steak and picked my prizewinning breading off it—it won first prize six years in a row at the Venice Founders' Day Festival, and he won't touch it." She shuddered. "I told him this diet isn't healthy, but he won't listen." Of course, Wilda had her own interpretation of *healthy*. If she'd invented a food pyramid, it would have everything deep fried on the bottom, a layer of pies and cakes, a layer of coffee, and a layer of raw vegetables at the very top in the "use sparingly" category.

The bells at the entrance to the diner jingled and a dark form appeared in the doorway. It was Gus. At least, it was a form that somewhat resembled Gus. I'd never seen him look this awful before: he was pale and unshaven, and his hair stuck out in strange directions from his bald spot. He had dark circles under his eyes and looked like he hadn't slept all weekend. He hovered in the doorway, glanced over at us, and then tripped as he started to make his way over to our booth. Betty yowled and shot across the diner like a cannonball. Gus shouted a string of expletives.

"Watch your mouth! There are young people in this diner!" Wilda yelled at him.

He brushed himself off and leaned against the doorway. "You gotta get rid of that cat." He wagged his finger at Betty. "It's a health hazard. Fleabag vermin in a restaurant . . . oughta be a law against that. I'm gonna file a formal complaint with the Chamber of Commerce when I get a chance."

His speech was slurred; his eyes were bright red.

"You do that, Gus," Wilda said.

"I'm going to," he said. "Don't think I won't."

Wilda rolled her eyes and made the rounds with the coffeepot. Sam and I rushed over to him.

"Are you okay?" I asked.

He grunted, put a hand to his forehead, and rubbed his eyes. I could smell the alcohol on him. "Look, girls, I'm not really up for this. I'm going back home," he said.

"Are you all right?" Sam asked. "You didn't show up for work Friday, and . . ." Her voice trailed off.

"I'll call you tomorrow," Gus said.

Sam and I didn't know what else to say. We watched him turn and limp off down the sidewalk.

When he was out of sight, I asked Sam, "What's wrong with him? I've never seen him look this bad before."

Sam shook her head. "I don't know. He started acting weird on Thursday. He was in the worst mood and kept growling orders at me for no reason, then finally apologized and said he didn't feel well, and went home early. Then he didn't show up Friday, and this morning was the first time he picked up the phone. He sounded a little better then, like he was looking forward to meeting us tonight."

Wilda put the coffeepot back on the counter and started wiping it down. She'd heard our conversation and was smiling artificially, as if there was something she wasn't telling us.

"Do you know what's wrong with Gus?" I asked her.

She paused. "Mmmm," she grunted.

"What?" Sam asked. "What's going on?"

"Well—" She moved to the cash register and ran her finger over the Frolicking Felines calendar beside it. Each month showed a picture of a cat in different outfits; November was a tabby in a spacesuit. She rested her finger on Thursday, November 6, three days before.

"Yup, just what I thought," she said. She lowered her voice and spoke out of the corner of her mouth. "Thursday was *jick joookins* birthday."

"What?" I asked. She'd whispered the name so quietly I couldn't make out what she said.

She looked around to make sure no one was listening, and then waved us toward a deserted booth on the other side of the diner.

"It was Jack Jenkins's birthday," Wilda said.

"Who?" Sam asked.

Wilda folded her hands. "Gus's son."